Murder in Little Firling – Omnibus Volume One

The Little Firling Murder Mysteries:

Books 1–3

By Belinda Chavremootoo

Dedication

For every cat who ever solved a mystery

quietly before the humans caught up.

Text Copyright

About the Author

Belinda writes layered mysteries where memory lingers, landscapes remember, and silence speaks louder than words. Her stories slip between the literary and the intimate—part atmospheric suspense, part quiet reckoning. Rooted in a love for islands, history, and hidden truths, her work invites readers to linger in the in-between.

She believes some lands carry echoes of everything they've witnessed—grief, joy, betrayal—and that nostalgia for a place is its own kind of story.

She also writes heartfelt children's stories that whisper courage into quiet hearts. With magical ladybugs, story-saving oaks, and brave little girls like Maia, Belinda hopes to help young readers find their own voice—and use it boldly.

When she's not writing, Belinda tends to her garden, guided by the rustle of leaves, the smell of earth, and the quiet company of two cats who always seem to know more than they let on.

Little Firling

Volume's Contents

Book 1 – *Murder Over the Misty Cliffs*

Book 2 – *Murder Blooms at the Fair*

Book 3 – *Murder Beneath the Ballroom Chandelier*

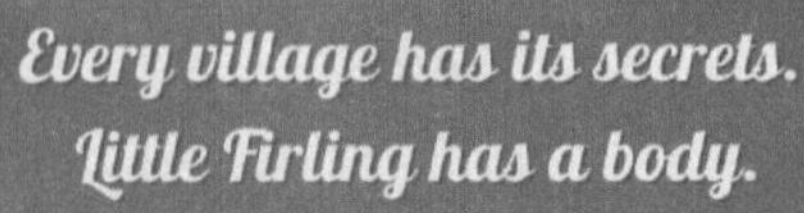

Every village has its secrets.
Little Firling has a body.

Murder Over the Misty Cliffs

A Little Firling Mystery - Book One

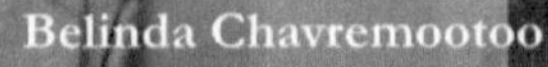

Belinda Chavremootoo

Table of Contents

Prologue - A Note on Little Firling 1

Chapter 1 4

Chapter 2 16

Chapter 3 22

Chapter 4 34

Chapter 5 46

Chapter 6..55

Chapter 7..69

Chapter 8..79

Chapter 9..89

Chapter 10..97

Chapter 11..105

Chapter 12..113

Chapter 13..119

Chapter 14..127

Chapter 15..135

Chapter 16..144

Chapter 17..152

Chapter 18..159

Chapter 19..168

Prologue - A Note on Little Firling

(as observed by Annabel Lennox Deighton, late 50s, reluctant detective)

Little Firling is the kind of place you escape to.

Crumbling cliffs. Rolling green fields. A sea that never quite tells you what it's thinking. It's beautiful, of course — wildly, wind-whipped beautiful — but also just mysterious enough to feel like something's always watching from behind the hydrangeas.

The village itself leans into the charm. Ivy-draped cottages. A pub with the original crooked sign. Bunting for events no one truly remembers. Everyone knows your name, your birthday, and the last three things you bought from Bea Simmons' bakery — and they're not afraid to bring any of those up over a cup of tea.

When I moved here from Glasgow after retiring early, I expected peace and maybe a few curious glances. What I got was a cat with the gaze of a magistrate, a best friend who carries a baseball bat "just in case," and a murder investigation I had no business leading — except, apparently, I did.

Because Little Firling has its secrets. Old ones. The kind you trip over while gardening. The kind whispered through generations until someone — usually someone like me — decides to dust them off.

So, if you're here for a peaceful coastal escape?

You might get your wish.

Just... don't go wandering near the cliffs after dark.

Chapter 1

The mist crept in with the confidence of an old friend. It wrapped around the chimney pots and pressed up against the windows of Honeystone Cottage like it knew exactly where the warmth was. It blurred the horizon until land and sea became whispers of each other, and it made Annabel Lennox Deighton feel—for the first time in a long time—quiet.

Not numb. Not empty. Just... quiet.

She stood at the edge of the clifftop path, boots sunk into damp grass, one gloved hand resting lightly on the worn wooden gate that marked the end of her new garden and the beginning of the great, green beyond. The sea murmured below, distant and restless, like it was having an argument with itself.

Persephone, her black Bombay cat, rubbed against her calf; a warm velvet coil of black fur and quiet judgment. She chirped—a soft, questioning sound—and Annabel looked down.

"Still not sure what we're doing here, are you?" she murmured.

The cat blinked up at her, golden eyes round and solemn. Another soft sound. Not quite agreement. Not quite disapproval.

"I know. Same."

It had been almost a month since she had left Glasgow behind. A city filled with friends, colleagues, and noise—so much noise—and the increasingly empty flat where Michael's books still lived on the shelves like polite ghosts. Two years of widowhood had passed like weather: sometimes stormy, sometimes still, always somewhere else. She had taught two more terms after he died, out of habit more than purpose. Then one day, she had stopped. Packed up her lecture notes, cancelled the dinner parties she had not wanted to attend, and bought a stone cottage in a village she had never heard of until it appeared in a Google search at 2:00 a.m.

Little Firling. She had liked the sound of it.

Quiet. Seaside. Not too far from a train line. The sort of place where people grew things.

Persephone had come, naturally. You did not leave behind your only living confidante—even if she had a habit of talking back in chirps and blinks and never let you drink tea without inspecting the cup first.

They walked the cliffs every morning now. Part ritual, part meditation. It was becoming a habit—one of the first she had chosen for herself in a long time.

The fog thickened as they walked, the sea vanishing behind it. Persephone trotted ahead, then stopped. Her ears pricked forward. She let out a sharper chirp and darted into the scrub just off the path.

Annabel frowned. "Another vole?" No answer.

She followed.

It took a moment to find her—sitting perfectly still beside something low and crumpled in the grass.

At first, it looked like a pile of old coats. Something someone had dropped and forgotten.

Then she saw the shoe.

Then the still hand.

Then the open eyes.

Annabel's breath caught. Persephone sat beside the figure; tail wrapped neatly around her paws.

The man was slumped against a moss-covered boulder. His face pale. His mouth slightly open. No sign of violence. No blood. Just... stillness.

And at his side, caught in the brambles, a notebook. Its cover warped by moisture, its pages fluttering weakly in the breeze like it was trying to breathe.

Annabel crouched.

She did not touch the body.

But she did reach for the notebook.

It was damp, but not ruined—just barely legible in parts. She turned it over carefully.

She turned the first page.

Symbols. Scribbles. A drawing of something that looked like the sun, with three stars circling it. Strange, urgent handwriting.

She hesitated. Then slid it gently into her satchel, already imagining it in one of the plastic bags in her kitchen drawer.

"If it's important," she murmured to herself, *"I'd rather it not disappears."*

Persephone let out one, low meow. Quiet, like a warning.

Annabel stood slowly.

There was something here. Not just a body. A story.

And she had walked right into the middle of it.

She returned to the cottage after calling the authorities. PC Tom Oakes—helpful, if slightly over-eager—had promised to "come up sharpish" and "sort it all out." Whatever that meant.

Now, she stood in the centre of her small garden, fingers wrapped around a steaming mug of tea, Persephone perched on the low stone wall as if she were conducting surveillance.

Honeystone Cottage was exactly what it had promised to be: a little crooked, a little magical. Roses curled around the front windows like gossip, the paint on the door was a cheerful but chipped blue, and the back garden sloped toward the fields in a lazy, uneven sprawl. Someone, once, had tried to tame it. The bones of an herb patch remained—old thyme clumps, stubborn mint, even a half-wild rosemary bush that smelled of forgotten dinners.

Annabel was already planning what to plant. Courgettes. Lavender. Marigolds, maybe.

She needed something to grow.

"I brought scones, but I can leave them on the step if this is a no-socializing sort of morning."

The voice came from behind her— bright, brash, unapologetically alive.

Annabel turned.

The woman in the patchwork coat and sturdy boots looked like she could win a bar fight and still make it to book club with jam on her sleeve. Her red hair was in an unapologetic twist, her eyes sharp and curious.

"Evie Barnes," she said, holding out a Tupperware. "Bookshop, gossip, occasionally foul-mouthed first responder to village drama. And you're the professor with the cat and the aura of heartbreak."

Annabel blinked.

Evie grinned. "Too much?"

"Just unexpected," Annabel said, taking the container. "I'm Annabel."

"I know. We've been watching you."

"Who's 'we'?"

Evie pointed vaguely toward the village. "Everyone. It's how we welcome people. With food and mild surveillance."

Annabel raised an eyebrow.

Evie gestured toward Persephone. "She's been giving my Labrador the death glare through the hedge."

"She's not fond of dogs."

"Neither am I, but I don't stare at them like they owe me money."

Annabel smiled. A real one, the first in a while.

They stood quietly for a moment, the mist curling around the roses, the fields yawning open behind them.

Then Annabel said, "There's been a body. On the cliffs."

Evie did not gasp.

She just said, "Right. Tea first, then crime-solving. You've moved to the right village."

Chapter 2

The fog had thinned, but it had not left.

It clung to the hedgerows like a sulking child, reluctant to release the morning entirely. The path to the cliffs felt softer underfoot, the grass still damp. Annabel walked steadily, Persephone's absence at her heels oddly noticeable.

In her satchel was a Ziploc bag containing the notebook.

She had cleaned it gently, just enough to stop the pages from warping further. It felt wrong to hold it—like touching something meant for someone else. But worse, it had felt wrong to leave it behind.

As she neared the edge of the cliffs, she saw the familiar fluorescent pop of PC Tom Oakes' jacket.

"Professor Deighton," he called, waving. "Glad you made it back."

Annabel nodded, her eyes flicking toward the body—still untouched, respectfully marked by police tape and a few cones that looked like they had been borrowed from the primary school.

"Didn't want to move anything until someone confirmed what they saw," Oakes said. "This him, then? Ernie Finch?"

"Yes," she said quietly.

She opened her satchel and held out the notebook in the Ziploc.

"He was clutching this. I thought it might be important."

Oakes took it, squinted through the plastic, then gave a half-shrug.

"Looks like diagrams. Scribbles. Probably just academic notes. He was always rambling about shipwrecks and old legends, wasn't he?"

He handed it back without even opening it.

Annabel did not move. "He was holding it. Tight."

"Could've been reflex. People grip things as they fall."

"But his body wasn't in a position that looked like a fall," she said. "His legs were crossed. His shoulders were slumped. He looked... arranged."

Oakes blinked. "I'll mention that to the coroner. But no visible signs of trauma. No wounds, no bruising. Might've been a heart attack."

Annabel did not respond. Her gaze drifted back to Ernie's face.

He had not looked peaceful.

He had looked like he was *waiting for something.*

Or someone.

"Still," Oakes continued, scribbling in a half-folded notepad. "Nothing alarming. If anything turns up in the autopsy, I'll let you know."

Annabel nodded, but something inside her stayed rigid.

He did not ask about the notebook again.

***

Back at Honeystone Cottage, the kettle was already whistling when she stepped through the door.

Persephone blinked at her from the table, then stared directly at the notebook as she placed it down, still sealed. The cat gave one soft chirp. Judgemental.

"I agree," Annabel muttered, putting the kettle off. "That wasn't satisfying at all."

There was a knock at the door.

Evie.

She stood holding a pastry bag and two steaming takeaway cups like a caffeinated storm cloud.

"I figured you needed backup. I brought pastries and nosiness."

Annabel stepped aside. "Come in."

Chapter 3

The notebook lay between them like a loaded question.

Annabel turned another page, careful not to tear the dampened edge. The paper crackled slightly, but the ink was still mostly legible. It was all there: sketches, symbols, notes scribbled sideways in the margins. One page was entirely dedicated to what looked like shipping codes—numbers arranged in vertical rows, underlined three times at the top with the words:

CRATE ELEVEN — MISSING?

Customs forms don't match. Hale. Cooke.

Annabel leaned over her cup of tea. "Cooke. That's... Maggie Cooke?"

Evie nodded slowly.

"And Hale," Evie added, "as in Rupert Hale. Landlord to half the village, including your cottage previously. And owner of the old mill, the chapel, and three 'historically preserved' sheds no one can explain."

Annabel turned another page. The symbol appeared again—the sun with three stars, scrawled repeatedly beside the word *'hidden'* and a rough sketch of the cliff path.

"This wasn't research," she said. "This was a warning."

Evie was quiet for a moment. Then: "You still think this was murder?"

Annabel looked at the notebook. "Yes. I think he was trying to tell someone something before it was too late."

Persephone meowed softly from the windowsill and stretched, her tail twitching once.

"Her Highness agrees," Evie muttered. "Right. I'm going to dig through my aunt's archive box. If she knew anything about this symbol, it'll be in there. She hoarded papers like other people hoard plastic bags."

Annabel stood to refill the kettle when there was a knock at the door.

"Expecting someone?" Evie asked.

"No."

She opened the door.

Maggie Cooke stood on the step, her cheeks flushed and a waxed paper bag in her hands.

"Hello, love. I just thought—you probably haven't had a proper lunch, with everything this morning and all. Brought some Cornish pasties round. Fresh out the oven." She offered a smile that was a little too bright.

Annabel hesitated. "That's very kind."

"Just trying to help where I can," Maggie said, stepping into the hallway without waiting. "Oh hello, Evie. Still poking about in things, you shouldn't, I, see?"

Evie smiled with zero warmth. "That's the job title, more or less."

Maggie handed Annabel the warm bag, eyes darting around the kitchen.

And then—very briefly—she spotted the notebook.

Just sitting there, on the table, next to the mugs and sugar pot.

Her gaze froze on it for half a second. She didn't say anything.

But she didn't need to.

She knew what it was.

"Oh," she said too casually. "Is that Ernie's handwriting?"

Annabel's heart gave a single hard thump.

"I thought no one had identified the man yet," she said quietly.

Maggie blinked. "Oh. Did I say Ernie? I—someone in the bakery mentioned seeing him yesterday. Near the cliffs. I assumed it might be..."

She trailed off.

Evie crossed her arms.

Maggie quickly turned back to Annabel. "Anyway, I should get back. Busy day, even with... you know. Best not to let things slip just because of a little excitement."

She was out the door before either of them could respond.

***

"She didn't ask about the body," Evie said.

"No."

"She didn't ask what we saw."

"No."

"But she knew it was Ernie."

Annabel set the pasties down and walked slowly back to the table. Her fingers hovered just above the notebook, as though it might vanish.

"I don't think she came here to check on me," she said.

Persephone chirped again.

Unbothered.

"I need to get some things from the shop," Annabel added. "Tea. Milk. Sugar.

Spices for cooking. I love experimenting with world cuisine and this type of cooking helps me relax and find inspiration."

She paused for a moment, then added with a playful glint in her eye, "And perhaps I'll come up with some subtle questions, the kind that people answer without realizing they're being gently probed. It's always fascinating to uncover little truths about people."

Evie grinned. "My favourite kind."

***

The village was already humming with gossip.

Annabel passed two women from the Women's Institute (WI) whispering beside the post-box. The grocer gave her a sympathetic smile he clearly reserved for people who had *"seen things."* Mr. Wilkins waved half-heartedly as his dachshund barked at her ankles like it was trying to banish evil spirits.

At the shop, the conversation shifted the moment she stepped through the door.

"Oh hello, Professor," chirped Kitty Simmons from the garden centre, suddenly *extremely* interested in a box of shortbread. "Terrible news, this morning, just awful. And so soon after moving in."

Annabel offered a nod. "Small villages have large reactions."

"Was it true?" Kitty asked, lowering her voice. "That he was holding something? A coin? Or a diary?"

Annabel blinked. "Where did you hear that?"

Kitty flushed. "Oh, you know... word gets around."

Annabel paid for her groceries and left without another word.

***

She returned to the cottage twenty minutes later.

Everything looked normal.

The door was locked. The windows unbroken. Persephone was stretched out on the windowsill, a small white feather trapped under one paw like a trophy.

Annabel smiled faintly and stepped inside.

She put the groceries down. Pulled off her coat. Walked into the kitchen.

Stopped.

The notebook was gone.

She looked around—every surface, every drawer, every cupboard. No sign of it. No mess. No break-in. Nothing.

Persephone jumped down from the window and landed softly at her feet.

Annabel stared at the table, her heart thudding.

Who even had access?

And then it clicked.

Rupert Hale had mentioned it casually when she signed the lease: "Maggie's been helping out for years. Goes in to air the place, do a little clean now and then. Hope that's alright. She's very trustworthy."

Maggie had not asked to use the loo.

She hadn't looked around the kitchen like it was new.

She had not needed to.

Annabel turned toward the door, jaw tightening.

Persephone meowed once.

Not surprised.

Chapter 4

The morning light filtered through the lace curtains of Honeystone Cottage like a secret trying to sneak in. Annabel stood at the kitchen table, staring at the spot where the notebook had been.

Gone. Cleanly. Silently.

Persephone was perched in its place, her sleek black form coiled neatly, golden eyes unblinking.

"I know," Annabel murmured. "I should've hidden it better."

The cat didn't move. But her tail tapped once against the table, a soft reprimand.

Annabel turned toward the phone and dialled the bookshop.

Evie picked up on the second ring. "If this is about the postmistress calling you 'our new Jessica Fletcher,' I already yelled at her."

"It's not that," Annabel said. "The notebook's gone."

Silence.

Then: "Did someone break in?"

"No. The door was locked. Nothing else touched. I was out for maybe twenty minutes."

Another pause. "So, someone with a key."

Annabel nodded, even though Evie couldn't see her. "I think it was Maggie."

"Tea. Your place. Twenty minutes."

Click.

***

By the time Evie arrived, Annabel had unpacked the groceries she had bought the day before—the lemons, saffron, cinnamon, preserved lemon, and dried apricots.

"What's this?" Evie asked.

"Lunch. Peace offering. Interrogation tool."

"You're weaponizing tagine?"

Annabel smiled faintly. "It's worked before."

As she cooked, the kitchen filled with warmth and spice, memories curling up in the steam. She had not made this dish since Michael passed. He used to say the smell made the flat feel like a Moroccan courtyard instead of a rainy street in Glasgow.

Persephone remained by her feet the entire time, alert, watchful, more clingy than usual.

"She knows something's off," Annabel said.

Evie sipped her tea. "So do we."

***

The three of them—Annabel, Evie, and Persephone—made their way down the lane to Maggie Cooke's cottage. The basket was warm in Annabel's arms. The cat followed at a polite but determined distance, tail high like a tiny black banner of suspicion.

Maggie answered the door after the second knock. Her hair was pinned up in a lopsided bun, her apron stained with flour. She looked surprised to see them.

"Oh! I—good morning."

"We thought you might enjoy something savoury for a change," Annabel said, lifting the basket. "I made tagine."

Maggie hesitated. Then stepped aside. "Well, how can I say no to that?"

***

The kitchen was warm and smelled faintly of sugar and something more floral—rosewater, maybe. There were scones cooling near the window and an old radio humming from the corner.

As soon as they stepped inside, Persephone paused on the threshold.

Her nose twitched.

She stared directly at a teacup on the counter.

Then, without sound or ceremony, she sat. Ears forward. Eyes narrowed.

Annabel glanced down. "Something wrong, girl?"

Persephone didn't move. She was alert, focused—locked in.

Annabel's eyes followed her gaze.

Rosewater.

The exact scent that had lingered in the cottage the morning the notebook vanished.

She met Evie's eyes.

Evie raised a brow.

They both turned to Maggie.

***

Lunch was served in awkward silence.

The tagine was well received—Maggie complimented the flavour, the tenderness of the chicken—but her eyes kept darting between the women like she expected them to say something. Or perhaps she was waiting for them *not* to.

Finally, Annabel said gently, "You knew what Ernie was researching."

Maggie's fork paused mid-air.

"I didn't take anything," she said.

"We never said you did," Evie replied, setting down her glass of water. "But it's interesting you knew something was missing."

Maggie's hands dropped into her lap. "Ernie talked too much. He thought he was onto something big. He showed me drawings... pages from shipping logs."

"Did they mention your family?" Annabel asked.

Maggie's jaw tightened. "He believed the wreck was planned. That certain families profited while others died. My great-grandfather died on *The Golden Mare*. My grandmother always said he was an honest man. Ernie made it sound like he'd been a pawn. Or worse."

"So, you were protecting him?" Annabel said softly.

"I was protecting *them*," Maggie said. "The people who came after. Who didn't ask to inherit shame."

Evie leaned forward. "Did you take the notebook?"

"No," Maggie whispered. "But I wish I had."

She stood abruptly, collected the plates, and turned her back to them.

Persephone moved to the edge of the table, never taking her eyes off the cupboard near Maggie's feet.

There was something under there. Something the cat could smell. Something that didn't belong.

Annabel rose. "Thank you for the conversation. And the tea."

Maggie didn't turn.

They left without another word.

***

Outside, the air felt heavier.

Persephone trotted ahead, her tail flicking like a metronome of judgment.

"She's lying," Evie muttered.

"She's scared," Annabel replied. "But yes."

"And the notebook?"

"I don't know. But Persephone does."

They walked in silence. The breeze carried the smell of rosemary and salt.

Somewhere behind them, in a cottage that smelled faintly of rosewater and regret, a woman washed three plates she had not

finished eating from.

Chapter 5

They walked in silence.

Gravel crunched beneath their boots as they left Maggie's cottage, the scent of rosewater clinging to their clothes like something unfinished.

Evie shoved her hands into her coat pockets. "Well, that was... awkward."

Annabel gave a slow nod. "She didn't deny anything. Not convincingly."

"But she didn't admit it either. I don't know what was more obvious—her fear, or the fact that she wanted us to leave."

Persephone padded ahead of them, her tail flicking like a tiny black lie detector.

She hadn't taken her eyes off Maggie's door until they were halfway home.

"She's scared," Annabel said. "And I think it's because the notebook... if she took it, she doesn't have it anymore."

Evie raised an eyebrow. "So, either she passed it on, or she hid it."

"She looked like someone who regrets trusting the wrong person," Annabel murmured.

***

Back at the bookshop, Evie pulled a dusty box from a top shelf and set it down on the counter with a sigh. "My aunt's archive. I kept it thinking it was WI gossip and biscuit recipes but it may contain something linked to the research that Ernie was doing."

Annabel opened it carefully. Inside were envelopes, old newspaper clippings, and notes written in a decisive hand.

Evie flipped through them. "She catalogued everything. Local families, land transfers, even crop rotations. Wait—here."

A sheet marked "*The Golden Mare – 1891*". A list of names. At the bottom, written in pen:

"*They split it. And someone paid the price.*"

Annabel's eyes landed on one name: Elias Hale. It was underlined three times.

Evie frowned. "That's Rupert's family."

Annabel leaned in. "He owns half the village now. Including the cottage that I bought from him and am now living in."

Evie glanced down at the note. "But why lie? Why act so scared about something that happened in 1891?"

Annabel's voice was low. "Because some legacies don't stay buried. The profit from that wreck didn't vanish—it was passed down. Quietly."

Evie crossed her arms. "And if someone like Maggie stumbled onto that truth..."

"They'd want her quiet," Annabel said.

They looked at each other.

"We should go back," Annabel said quietly. "Make sure she's alright."

Persephone meowed once, already sitting at the door like she had expected this.

***

Maggie's cottage looked just as it had earlier—but somehow, more still.

The curtains were drawn. One of the potted lavender plants had tipped over. The kitchen window glowed, but the light inside did not feel warm. It felt like a stage set—waiting for the next act.

Annabel knocked.

No answer.

"Maggie?" she called.

Evie peered in through the side window. Her voice dropped. "There's something on the floor."

Persephone crouched low beside the doorstep; ears flattened. She did not meow.

Annabel tried the handle.

It opened.

***

The scent hit them instantly—burnt sugar, something floral, and something sharp and sour underneath it all.

"Maggie?" Annabel stepped into the kitchen.

Then they saw her.

She was collapsed on the floor, one arm reaching toward the chair, the other limp at her side. Her eyes were closed, her skin too pale. No blood. No obvious injury.

Annabel dropped to her knees. "She's breathing. Weak, but steady."

Evie pulled out her phone, fingers already dialling. "Calling an ambulance."

Annabel scanned the room. Nothing else was out of place.

No signs of forced entry. No broken glass. Her purse and jewellery were untouched.

"This wasn't a robbery," she said.

Then she saw it—a scorched corner of notebook paper peeking out from under the cupboard Maggie had slumped against.

Persephone darted forward, crouched, and tapped it toward Annabel with a soft thwap of her paw.

Annabel picked it up carefully. The edges were burned; the ink smeared—but one line was still visible:

"Not just about the gold..."

She looked down at Maggie. Then to Evie.

"She let someone in," Annabel said quietly. "Someone she thought she could trust."

Evie's jaw tightened. "And they took it?"

"Maybe," Annabel said. "Or maybe… they took something she said."

Her voice dropped further.

"What Maggie knew might not have been in the notebook at all."

Chapter 6

The air in Little Firling had changed.

Annabel felt it the moment she and Evie stepped into the village. It was in the way curtains twitched a second too long, how greetings were clipped, and conversations paused just long enough to mark a shift.

Persephone followed at their heels with focused grace, her black coat sleek as ink, her golden eyes taking everything in.

The village was humming—not with activity, but with tension.

***

They passed Ronnie Parkes, the postman, who tipped his cap like a man hiding dynamite in his mailbag. "Morning," he said, then added in a conspiratorial tone, "Heard Maggie's still unconscious. Funny thing... some folks sent flowers before the hospital even released the news."

He gave a wink and shuffled off with all the subtlety of a marching band.

Evie raised an eyebrow. "Did he just gossip in Morse code?"

Annabel smirked. "I think that was a yes, a warning, and a mild threat disguised as a compliment."

***

First stop: Kitty's Garden Shop, where she was bullying a tray of winter pansies into an arrangement, they clearly resented.

"Oh, Maggie, bless her heart," Kitty chirped without turning. "Terrible business. I do hope it wasn't something... dramatic."

Annabel tilted her head. "Did she ever talk to you about Ernie?"

Kitty paused for a fraction of a second. "Oh, he was always about, wasn't he? Maps and muttering. Said he was working on something *big*. Local history and all that."

Evie said nothing, but Persephone sneezed pointedly from the path.

"Charming creature," Kitty said through her teeth.

✳✳✳

Further down the lane, Felix Barlow was repositioning a flyer with the energy of someone trying to erase history with a staple gun.

"Still poking around?" he asked, without looking up. "Hoping for some literary closure?"

"We're just trying to understand what Ernie was working on," Annabel said.

Felix rolled his eyes. "He was chasing fairy tales. Crate Eleven, lost gold, ghost maps."

Evie stepped closer. "Didn't you write about the Golden Mare in the village quarterly?"

"I write about facts," Felix snapped. "Not pub fantasy."

He stomped off in the direction of nowhere, arms stiff.

As they walked toward the pub, Annabel murmured, "He's in the photo."

Evie blinked. "Felix?"

"On Maggie's fridge. That group photo. Kitty. Rupert. Penfold, sort of behind the trellis."

"That wasn't just a garden party," Evie said. "That was a roster."

"A roster of secrets," Annabel replied.

They passed the sea wall, where the beach was nearly deserted except for one figure.

Graham Hargreaves, long coat snapping in the wind, headphones on, methodically sweeping his metal detector.

"He's always out here," Evie said. "If anyone can find a bent coin from 1863 or a nail from the Norman invasion, it's Graham."

They watched as Graham Hargreaves paused mid-sweep on the beach, crouched, and carefully dug something from the sand.

He stared at it for a long moment, then started walking up the slope toward them.

Evie muttered, "That's new. Usually, he vanishes like a cryptid after he finds something."

Graham stopped in front of them, wind tousling his grey hair beneath a battered wool cap. He held out a small cloth pouch.

"Thought you might want this," he said.

Annabel took it gently. Inside, a coin — old, dulled by age, and etched with a pattern she did not immediately recognize. Around the edges were tiny marks that might've once been letters... or symbols.

"It's beautiful," she said. "Do you know where it's from?"

Graham shrugged. "Didn't find it. It found me."

He turned to go, then paused. "Not everything buried wants to stay that way."

Persephone sniffed at the pouch, then looked up at Graham with what could only be described as solemn approval.

"Thanks, Graham," Annabel said.

He did not respond. Just walked off toward the far rocks, metal detector swinging like a pendulum of fate.

Evie nudged her. "Well, that wasn't ominous at all."

Annabel tucked the pouch into her bag. "Let's just hope it's a clue, not a curse."

Persephone's ears twitched.

"Another whisper from the past," Annabel murmured.

***

The *Hare & Hound* was warm, dim, and murmuring with low conversation. The smell of ale and Sunday roasts lingered in the wood.

Henry Griggs, the bartender, gave them a solemn nod. "Back corner's quiet."

Persephone leapt onto her usual stool with aristocratic flair.

"Sardine pâté?" Henry asked.

She chirped once.

Confirmed.

Evie shook her head. "She's got better table service than I do."

"Don't take it personally," Henry said. "She tips in glares."

***

At a nearby table, Bertie the Butcher leaned in close to Bea Simmons, who was nursing a cider.

"I always said Kitty's smile was too wide," Bertie muttered.

"Wider than her herb beds," Bea agreed.

"And Felix? He's hiding something. Probably under those awful elbow patches."

In the corner, Frankie the Fisherman nursed a pint and muttered to himself, "Sea doesn't forget. It remembers. And it waits."

Two seats down, Tobias Marsh stared into his mug like it held the past.

"He was after Crate Eleven," Toby said softly.

Annabel turned to him. "Ernie?"

"Aye. Same as the rest, but louder. Wouldn't stop asking."

Evie leaned in. "Did he find anything?"

Toby tapped the rim of his mug. "My grandfather left a letter. Said the wreck wasn't an accident. Said some things came ashore that shouldn't have."

Annabel's eyes lit up. "Do you still have it?"

"Locked away," Toby said. "And staying there until I know it's safe."

He returned to silence like a drawbridge closing.

***

Near the fireplace, Mrs. Penfold clinked her glass against Bea's. "I told them if Ernie kept sniffing around, he'd end up like Florence Kemp's archive—dusty, unread, and full of things better left alone."

Annabel perked up. "Florence Kemp?"

Evie nodded. "Florie. Former librarian. Still keeps the real archive in her cottage.

The kind with actual index cards and handwritten side notes. She doesn't lend. She *guards*."

"Ernie was there?" Annabel asked.

"More than once," Penfold said. "Whatever he asked her, it rattled something."

***

Outside, dusk had painted the village rooftops in deepening blues.

Persephone hopped off her stool and padded ahead. Henry silently wiped her dish like it was part of the routine.

Annabel tightened her scarf.

"Tomorrow," she said, "we visit Florie Kemp."

"With or without an appointment?" Evie asked.

"With Persephone," Annabel replied. "No one denies her access."

Chapter 7

The next morning broke misty and cool, the kind of grey Cornish hush that made secrets feel just a little louder.

Annabel adjusted the strap of her satchel, stuffing in a notepad, her reading glasses, and three carefully worded conversation openers. Evie showed up ten minutes early with coffee and a grin.

"She's not exactly friendly," Evie warned as they walked. "She once refused to lend a book to the vicar because he returned another book with a biscuit crumb in the spine."

"And yet," Annabel said, "you think she'll let us look at her private archive?"

Evie held up a small foil container. "I brought her peppermint creams."

Annabel smiled. "You came prepared."

"I also brought the real charm offensive." She looked down. "You coming, Princess?"

Persephone strolled out from under the hedge with all the calm authority of a woman who had never once paid rent.

***

Florie Kemp's cottage sat just on the edge of the village, tucked behind a tangle of hawthorn and climbing roses. It looked exactly like the kind of place where secrets were alphabetised and no one dared walk on the moss path.

Evie knocked twice. Then again.

They waited.

Nothing.

And then, slowly, the door creaked open — just enough for one sharp green eye to peer out.

"Yes?"

"Morning, Florie," Evie chirped. "You're looking radiant as always."

"I know you're lying. What do you want?"

"We've come with peppermint creams," Evie said, holding up the tin, "and a question about Ernie Liddel."

A pause.

Then the door opened a fraction wider. "Who's your friend?"

Annabel stepped forward. "Annabel Lennox Deighton. I live in the cottage that used to be owned by—"

"Yes, yes. The one Rupert keeps trying to gentrify."

Then Florie's gaze dropped.

To the black fur. The green-gold eyes. The cat, now sitting serenely at her doorstep like a judge awaiting testimony.

"Oh," Florie said. "Well. If she approves... come in."

***

The cottage smelled of peppermint, paper, and defiance. The walls were lined floor to ceiling with bookshelves—mismatched, overstuffed, lovingly catalogued in little handwritten tags.

A grandfather clock ticked somewhere in the back like it was judging everyone.

"Sit," Florie said, gesturing to a pair of antique chairs that looked firm enough to improve posture by force.

Persephone, naturally, hopped onto a low windowsill and immediately began cleaning one paw, signalling her quiet satisfaction.

"You said you had a question about Ernie?"

"We think he may have uncovered something important," Annabel said. "Connected to the Golden Mare. And to Maggie Cooke's collapse."

Florie sat, folding her hands. "He came to me twice. First time with questions. Second time with *evidence*."

Annabel and Evie exchanged a look. "What kind of evidence?"

Florie rose without a word and disappeared into the back room.

Persephone followed, tail swaying like she had been summoned to a council meeting.

When Florie returned, she held a small black notebook—leather-bound, aged, and tied shut with a piece of green twine.

"This," she said, "was his backup."

Evie blinked. "He had a backup?"

"He was smarter than people gave him credit for," Florie said. "He knew someone might take the original. Left this one with me. Told me not to say a word unless something happened to him."

Annabel took it carefully. The notebook was heavier than it looked. Weighted with worry.

"We believe he was pushed from the cliff," Annabel said gently.

Florie's mouth thinned. "Then you'd best read it. But not here. I don't want that thing in my house now that the story's moving."

"Moving?" Evie asked.

"Secrets don't stay still, dear. They pace."

Annabel slipped the notebook into her satchel.

Florie crossed her arms. "One more thing."

They turned.

"You're not the first ones to come asking about Crate Eleven."

"Who else?" Annabel asked.

Florie gave a slow, pointed smile.

"Someone in that photo on Maggie's fridge."

***

As they stepped out into the cold again, Persephone wound between Annabel's legs, then trotted ahead like she had just closed a case.

Evie exhaled. "We have the notebook."

"And we have a list of names," Annabel said.

Evie glanced at her. "So, what next?"

Annabel's eyes were sharp.

"We see what Ernie was trying to tell us."

Chapter 8

Back at Honeystone Cottage, the kettle was on, the curtains were drawn, and Persephone had claimed her preferred position — sprawled luxuriously across the arm of the sofa, watching Annabel and Evie with the air of a feline literary agent reviewing a risky manuscript.

Annabel untied the green twine from Ernie's backup notebook. The leather cover was worn, its corners soft from handling. The first page was blank, but the second held a single line in tidy, deliberate script:

"If they find this before I'm dead, it wasn't an accident."

Evie blinked. "Comforting."

Annabel turned the page. The handwriting was neat at first, gradually growing more frantic, as if written in haste or fear. The entries were dated, not consistently, but enough to form a timeline.

***

Notebook Excerpts:

June 3rd

Crate Eleven again. The manifest in the parish records is incomplete. Something was removed and covered up. Elias Hale's name is everywhere — but why so many redactions?

July 17th

Maggie says her grandmother remembered the night of the wreck. Lanterns on the cliffs. Not an accident. They lit the signal themselves. Who else knew?

August 2nd

Found the ledger. Old, water-damaged, but clear enough. Payments made *after* the wreck. Not rescue funds. Payouts. To villagers.

August 15th

Someone's been watching me.

August 29th

I left the ledger with someone safe. If they come for the notebook, at least there's a trail. I think it's someone close. From the photo. Always smiling.

Last Entry (undated)

There's something under the floor at the old mill. Hidden in the beams. I need to be sure. Then I'll go to Tobias. He has the letter. He *knows*.

***

Annabel closed the book slowly.

"The ledger's not here," she said. "He hid it. And he left the trail for us."

Evie frowned. "Someone from the photo. 'Always smiling.' Kitty?"

"She's a contender," Annabel said. "But so is Penfold. And Rupert."

"And Tobias," Evie added. "He's the next step. He has the letter Ernie was going to see."

Annabel stood. "Let's go."

Persephone flicked her tail as if to say *finally*, and hopped down.

***

Tobias Marsh's cottage stood a little off the high street, half-camouflaged in ivy and salt spray. The garden was wild, the gate swung crooked, and an old wooden chair sat permanently stationed outside like a retired lighthouse keeper.

Toby opened the door before they knocked.

"You're early," he said, not unkindly.

"Tea's already on."

They followed him in, ducking under low beams and the scent of dried herbs.

Persephone immediately found a sunny spot and began grooming.

"I wasn't going to show it," he said as he rummaged through a drawer.

"Not even to Ernie. But he was getting close. And now... well. I think he paid for that closeness."

He returned with a folded piece of thick paper, yellowed with age and tied with a faded red ribbon.

"This is from my grandfather," he said.

"He was a young man when the wreck happened. But he was there. He saw the lanterns on the cliffs."

Annabel took it with reverence.

＊＊＊

The Letter:

December 12th, 1891

I write this for no one but the truth. We lit the lanterns that night to pull the ship to shore. It wasn't chance. It was design. Elias Hale paid us — me, Jonah Rook, and Sam Griggs. Said the cargo was his by rights. Told us it was only gold, but I saw more. A chest. Heavy. Locked with a strange symbol on the latch.

After the wreck, he vanished the ledger. Said it was too dangerous. That someone else was watching. We never saw the chest again.

I fear I'll carry this weight into the grave.

***

Evie leaned back. "It's not just a theory anymore."

Annabel nodded slowly. "This proves the wreck was staged. That Elias Hale paid off villagers. That the artifact—whatever it was—disappeared."

Tobias scratched at his chin. "Ernie thought it was still out there. Said something about the mill."

"We'll check there," Annabel said. "But carefully."

She handed the letter back. "Thank you, Toby. This matters."

He gave a small nod. "Keep an eye on that cat. She sees more than you do."

Persephone blinked solemnly. Approved.

***

As they stepped out into the late afternoon light, Annabel looked down at her satchel.

"Now we have a name. A date. A chest. And a missing ledger."

"And a growing list of people in that photo," Evie added.

Annabel's expression sharpened. "Next, we find the artifact."

Persephone leapt onto the garden wall and looked back at them as if to say:

"What took you so long?"

Chapter 9

They arrived at the old mill just as the sun dipped below the horizon, bathing the valley in a strange half-light that felt borrowed from another time.

The building stood stubborn against the years — slate roof patched, walls weathered, door still hanging slightly askew. It had once processed grain. Now it processed whispers.

Evie adjusted her flashlight. "So, you think Ernie meant here?"

Annabel nodded. "He said something was under the floor. In the beams. If he was right... this is where Crate Eleven ends."

Persephone stalked ahead, stepping lightly over uneven flagstones like she had lived there in a past life. She paused by the door, turned back, and meowed once. The serious kind.

Evie blinked. "That sounded like a warning."

Annabel pushed the door open.

***

Inside, the air was cool and damp, filled with dust and old wood and the faint tang of sea air that somehow reached even this far inland. Light slanted through cracks in the boarded-up windows. Everything creaked.

The main floor was empty — except for old barrels, a rusted wheel, and shadows.

"So where do we start?" Evie whispered.

Annabel pointed to the far side. "The support beams. Look for anything unusual."

They split up. Persephone lingered near a row of floorboards, sniffing intently. She pawed once at a narrow crack.

Annabel knelt beside her.

The beam was worn, but one plank was darker than the rest. Smoother. As if it had been touched more often.

She ran her hand along it — then stopped. There, near the base, was a small indentation. Circular. About the size of a coin.

"Evie," she said softly. "I think I found something."

Evie came over, shining the flashlight. "Is that... a keyhole?"

"No." Annabel pulled the small pouch from her bag — the one holding the coin Graham had given her earlier that day.

She pressed it into the circle.

A soft *click.*

The plank shifted.

With a breath, they lifted it together.

***

Beneath the floor was a shallow compartment. Inside, wrapped in layers of oilcloth and tied with faded ribbon, was a leather-bound book.

Not a ledger. *The* ledger.

Evie exhaled. "We found it."

Annabel pulled it free, hands trembling just slightly.

She opened it slowly.

Pages and pages of transactions. Names. Sums of money. And in the margins, strange symbols — one of which matched the mark Ernie had copied in his notebook.

But then—another sound.

A footstep. Not theirs.

Behind them.

***

They froze.

Persephone hissed, low and razor-sharp.

Evie raised her torch.

The door creaked again.

Someone was there. Watching.

And then — gone. A shape slipping out into the fading light.

Evie sprinted to the doorway but saw only the last flicker of motion heading toward the trees.

"They were watching us," she said. "Maybe waiting."

Annabel clutched the ledger to her chest. "They know we have it now."

Persephone jumped onto a beam and glared at the door like she knew exactly who it was.

***

Outside, dusk had deepened. The village lights were flickering to life in the distance. The wind carried the sound of the sea and something colder beneath it.

"They'll come for this," Annabel said, holding the book.

Evie nodded. "Then we make sure it ends here."

Annabel looked to Persephone, who sat perched like a statue, tail flicking.

"Let them come," she said.

Chapter 10

They spread the ledger open on Annabel's kitchen table.

The book smelled of damp wood and something metallic, like ink and old guilt. Its pages were thick and textured, written in a sharp, slanted hand that demanded respect. Persephone sat at one corner of the table; eyes fixed on it like she expected it to hiss.

Annabel flipped to the earliest entries.

Evie leaned in. "These names... they're all villagers."

"Or ancestors of villagers," Annabel said. "And not just people from 1891. Look at the later entries — these go on for *decades.*"

Payment records. Meeting notes. The margins held the real secrets.

Scribbled in ink were phrases like:

"C11 secured. Ledger moved."
"Reinforce tunnel supports."
"Penfold warned again — loose lips."
"R. Hale arranging discretion."

Evie pointed to that last one. "That's *Rupert's* grandfather, isn't it?"

"Or possibly his father," Annabel said. "The Hales have always held the keys."

"And Penfold—wait." Evie flipped back a few pages. "Here. Felix Barlow's family. A 'J. Barlow' received payment after the wreck."

Annabel's expression darkened. "Kitty's family name is Simmons. Look here — 'B. Simmons — bakery stock cover, December 1891.'"

"Everyone in that photo," Evie said slowly, "has a connection to this book."

***

They made a list.

Each name. Each link. And a new question beside everyone.

By the end, the page was crowded:

Rupert Hale — estate ties, land ownership, connections to the old mill

Mrs. Penfold — family linked to communication and silencing dissent

Felix Barlow — possible rival historian or guardian of family shame

Kitty Simmons — cheery distraction or deliberate misdirection

Tobias Marsh — the letter, the witness

Bea Simmons — related to Kitty? Connected to the food ledger entries?

***

The doorbell rang.

They froze.

Evie peeked out the window.

"Speak of the devil," she muttered.

It was Rupert Hale.

Dressed impeccably. Hair just windswept enough to be trustworthy. Smiling like a man who did not just bury a village secret.

Annabel tucked the ledger beneath a dish towel and opened the door just a crack.

"Rupert," she said, voice cool.

"Annabel," he smiled. "Hope I'm not disturbing you. I was just dropping off a little something. You left this in the village shop."

He held out a slip of paper — a receipt. Harmless.

Too harmless.

"Thank you," she said, not reaching for it.

He did not leave.

Instead, he looked past her shoulder, eyes lingering on the kitchen table. His gaze flicked — once — to the covered book.

"You know," he said casually, "this village has a way of wrapping people up in its stories. You'll find that some are better left alone."

Annabel met his gaze. "And some are worth finishing."

His smile did not falter. But it no longer reached his eyes.

"Do let me know if you need anything," he said smoothly. "I always keep a spare key to your cottage. As a courtesy."

She shut the door before he finished the sentence.

Evie exhaled. "Subtle."

Persephone let out a low growl.

***

That evening, they locked every window.

The ledger went into a safe Annabel had almost forgotten she had, tucked behind her books on ancient detective fiction.

Persephone curled up on top of the safe.

Guarding it.

Like she understood everything.

And somewhere in the village, someone was already planning their next move.

Chapter 11

Rain whispered against the windows of Honeystone Cottage, the kind of slow, steady drizzle that blurred the world and made shadows linger.

The fire crackled softly. Persephone dozed on the windowsill... or at least pretended to. Her ears stayed twitching.

At the kitchen table, Annabel turned the pages of the ledger like it might bite.

"This handwriting changes here," she murmured.

Evie leaned over. "That's not Rook?"

"No. Different hand. More deliberate. Someone else took over."

They traced the entries. The earlier ones — hurried, anxious. The later ones — meticulous. Calm, even. But the content? Anything but.

***

May 1939

Rook is gone. Took his guilt with him. The gold still lingers. So do the lies.

October 1978

Hale's grandson is rising. Just like his father. He does not believe in ghosts — but he is one.

***

Annabel paused on the final page.

If you've found this, I'm no longer here...

I wrote because someone had to.

Let the truth breathe again.

—J.R.

❄❄❄

They sat in silence for a moment.

Then Evie said, quietly, "You realise we're holding the only copy of the truth."

Annabel nodded slowly. "And both it and Ernie's notebook are in my house."

She looked toward the front door, remembering Rupert's perfect smile — and the way his eyes had flicked, uninvited, toward her kitchen table.

"I always keep a spare key to your cottage..."

Her tea had gone cold.

Evie watched her. "Annabel... you don't think he followed us to the mill, do you?"

Annabel did not answer. Her mind was already racing.

Rupert had shown up far too soon after their discovery. No one *should* have known they had gone to the mill. But somehow, he did. And if he had a key to the cottage...

"Is it just Rupert?" Annabel whispered. "Or does anyone else have access?"

"Maggie," Evie said, hesitating. "Before she fell into that coma. She used to air the place out. Make sure it stayed liveable."

Persephone stirred, hopped down, and moved to the kitchen door. She sat. Still. Watching.

Evie followed her gaze.

"You locked that, right?"

Annabel nodded. "And the back one. But if someone *wanted* in—"

Evie stood. "We're moving the notebook and the ledger. Somewhere no one would look."

Annabel stared at the ledger for a long moment.

"It feels wrong," she said quietly. "This isn't just a mystery anymore. This is something people have killed to keep buried."

Evie crossed her arms. "And now it's on your kitchen table next to a fruit bowl."

They wrapped the ledger in an old jumper and slid it into the small wall safe hidden behind Annabel's row of vintage crime novels. The notebook went in, too. The dial clicked shut.

Persephone immediately leapt up and parked herself on the shelf above it.

Guarding.

As always.

***

Later, by the fire, Evie curled into the armchair with a blanket and a growing look of worry on her face.

Annabel stared into the flames.

"I'm not a detective," she murmured. "I was a literature professor. I used to read mystery novels. Now I'm living one. And I don't know where the line is anymore."

Evie looked up. "You know what I think? I think you were always meant to solve something bigger than fiction."

Annabel smiled, but it didn't quite reach her eyes. "I just didn't expect fiction to push back."

Outside, the rain turned to wind. A shutter clacked against the wall.

Annabel's gaze flicked toward the darkened windows.

"Whoever hid that ledger... they wanted us to finish this. But finishing it might mean waking up everything they tried to bury."

Evie raised her mug. "Then let's make sure we're the ones who write the last page."

Chapter 12

The Little Firling Spring Fair had always been the village's favourite form of mass distraction.

Bunting hung limp in the damp breeze, stalls lined the green, and the scent of sugared dough, sausage rolls, and wet grass clung to everything. There were children racing around the maypole, pensioners debating sponge textures, and somewhere — as always — Ronnie the postman was distributing gossip as naturally as flyers.

But this year? Something was off.

Too many eyes glanced. Too many smiles twitched too tight. The laughter felt performative, like the village was putting on a show it no longer believed in.

***

Annabel stood beside Evie at the tea tent, clutching paper cups of milky brew and eyeing the crowd like she was scanning an Agatha Christie cover.

"Rupert's not here," Evie said, sipping. "Which is weird, since he usually chairs the jam auction and praises everyone's lemon curd like it's gold-plated."

Annabel's gaze swept the green. "Neither's Kitty."

Evie frowned. "Kitty never misses a fair. She's the reason the 'best herb bundle' category even exists."

Persephone, nestled in her travel basket on the table behind them (highly illegal, absolutely unchallenged), let out a low, inquisitive *mrrrow.*

A warning.

Annabel turned just as Bea Simmons approached — cheeks red, apron dusted with flour, and eyes slightly too bright.

"Afternoon," she said, voice overly cheerful. "Lovely weather for it."

"Sure is," Evie replied dryly, glancing at the threatening sky.

Bea leaned closer, then dropped her voice. "You didn't hear this from me... but

Penfold's gone quiet. Cancelled her reading group. Says she's not feeling well."

Evie blinked. "She's never missed a Tuesday since 1989."

Bea nodded. "And Graham — hasn't been seen in two days."

Annabel stiffened. "What do you mean, not seen?"

"His mate from Penzance came looking for him this morning. Said he was supposed to meet him yesterday. Nothing."

Bea glanced around, then handed them a folded paper napkin.

"Found this under his usual stool at the Hare & Hound. Didn't tell Henry. Figured... you'd want it."

She disappeared into the crowd before they could ask more.

Annabel unfolded the napkin.

Inside was a note, written in frantic, cramped script.

They know I gave it to her.

I should have burned it.

I'm being watched.

If anything happens — look under the rusted wheel.

Evie whispered, "That's Graham's writing."

Annabel folded the note slowly.

"We need to go back to the mill."

As they stepped away from the fair, the clouds above darkened.

Back at the cottage, Persephone sat by the door, stiff, tail swishing.

"Someone was in the garden while we were gone," Evie said quietly, pointing to a fresh shoeprint near the herb patch.

Annabel's voice was steady. "They're warning us now."

Evie met her eyes. "Which means we're close."

Annabel nodded. "Too close."

Chapter 13

The mill was darker than they remembered.

The sky, now thick with rainclouds, had smothered the last of the spring light. What had once felt like a forgotten relic now felt... watched. As if the air itself was holding its breath.

Persephone leapt from Annabel's arms the moment they crossed the threshold, padding forward with silent authority. Her tail was raised, her steps slow and intentional.

Evie clicked on her torch. "You're sure it was *this* wheel?"

Annabel nodded. "Graham said, 'under the rusted wheel.' The only one left is the main gear by the support beams."

They moved across the creaking floorboards, careful to avoid the deeper cracks. The wheel sat in the far corner, half-collapsed, flanked by a stack of empty barrels and a wall of ivy-stained stone.

Annabel crouched beside it.

There it was — the same beam. The same faint indentation.

She pulled the cloth pouch from her coat pocket — the one Graham had handed her days before, the coin still nestled inside.

She pressed the coin into the groove.

Click.

A soft, mechanical *snick* echoed beneath the boards. A hidden panel shifted.

Evie stepped forward. "That never stops being creepy."

Together, they lifted the plank.

***

The smell of oilcloth and age rolled out like a whisper.

Inside, nestled in a shallow hollow, was a leather-bound book — thicker than Ernie's notebook, bound in cracked black leather, the edges worn smooth.

Annabel lifted it with care, as if the weight was not just physical.

Evie whistled. "That's not Ernie's. Is that...?"

Annabel nodded. "The ledger."

They opened it on a workbench in the far corner, where the torchlight would not catch through the gaps in the boards.

The pages were dense — names, dates, sums. Each line written with precision.

And then, halfway through, the handwriting changed.

***

May 1939

Rook is gone. Took his guilt with him. The gold still lingers.

June 1944

Children of the wreck men now hold the line. Some don't even know what they're protecting.

April 1962

They tried to destroy the book. I saved it. This copy is all that's left.

October 1978

Hale's heir is watching. Pretends not to see. But he knows.

***

Evie whispered, "There are two writers."

Annabel nodded. "Jonathan Rook started it. But someone else... someone who inherited it — finished it."

They reached the final page.

A different ink. A slower hand.

***

Final Entry

I kept the truth as long as I could. Hid it where it started. Let the wind guard it.

You may not know me. But if you're reading this... it means you were meant to.

Let the truth breathe again.

—J.R.

***

They stood in silence.

Even Persephone stopped her quiet patrolling and sat perfectly still by the door, as if keeping watch.

Annabel closed the book gently.

"We need to get this out of here."

Evie nodded. "Before someone else does."

They stepped out into the cool evening air, hearts heavier, feet faster.

Somewhere behind them, a floorboard creaked.

But when they turned — there was no one there.

Only the sound of the wind through broken rafters... and a soft meow from Persephone, low and warning.

Chapter 14

The rain had stopped, but the air clung damp and uneasy.

Back at Honeystone Cottage, the ledger sat sealed inside Annabel's small wall safe, tucked behind a row of vintage crime novels no one had touched in decades. Persephone, as ever, had resumed her post above it — like a sphinx with a grudge.

Evie made tea. Strong. No frills.

Neither of them said much. The silence wasn't awkward — it was *loading.*

Then—

Knock knock.

Two gentle, perfectly timed taps.

Annabel froze, teacup halfway to her lips.

Evie peered out the side window.

"Of course," she muttered. "It's Rupert."

Annabel sighed and set her cup down. "Let him in before he knocks again and starts chatting with the hydrangeas."

She opened the door.

And there he stood.

Rupert Hale — coat collar turned just enough to suggest drama, hair charmingly wind-tossed, eyes too knowing for comfort.

"Good afternoon," he said with that unshakeable grin. "Hope I'm not intruding."

Annabel stepped aside. "You usually are."

"Ah," he chuckled. "You always were sharper than most of our local imports."

Evie hovered in the kitchen; arms crossed. Not hostile. Just... prepared.

Rupert stepped inside, glancing once — and only once — toward the fireplace and the bookshelf beside it.

Annabel saw it. So did Persephone. Her tail flicked.

"I was just in the area," he said, sliding his gloves off. "Thought I'd check in. You've been... busy, haven't you?"

Annabel's voice was calm. "If you mean I attended the village fair, yes. I even had a slice of Bea Simmons' questionable cherry tart."

Rupert's smile didn't falter. "No, I meant the *other* kind of busy. The mill. Late walks. Curious conversations."

Evie bristled. "Is there a problem, Rupert?"

He turned. "Not at all. Just a gentle reminder that Little Firling has a way of *protecting its peace.* Some stories are best left in the pages where they belong."

Annabel stepped forward. "Some stories were never told properly to begin with."

A pause.

Then Rupert's gaze sharpened just slightly.

"I suppose I should mention," he said softly, "that I still have a spare key to this cottage. Bit of an oversight, really. From when it was in the family. Some habits... linger."

He smiled wider.

Annabel did not blink. "Then perhaps it's time to break those habits."

Rupert stepped back toward the door, brushing invisible lint from his sleeve.

"Well. I won't keep you."

He turned, hand on the knob.

"Oh," he added over his shoulder, "and if you do come across anything curious — old papers, family things — do let me know. I'd hate for something... sensitive to fall into the wrong hands."

He left.

The door clicked shut behind Rupert.

The silence that followed was heavier than it should've been.

Annabel walked slowly back to the window. The lane was empty now. The wind had picked up — just enough to rattle the trellis.

She pressed her fingers to the sill.

"You'd hate this, wouldn't you, Michael?" she thought. *"All this whispering and posturing. You'd roll your eyes and say it's not worth the drama. Then you'd make coffee and help me decode it anyway."*

The ache sat low in her chest — a familiar echo. Not sharp. Not gone.

She reached up and touched the spine of his old map book on the shelf. Still where she had left it. Unopened, but not forgotten.

"Well," she said aloud, voice steadying, "we're in it now."

Behind her, Persephone let out a low trill of agreement.

Then Evie exploded: "He's practically *yelling* that he knows we have it!"

Persephone growled low and deep. No fluff. All warning.

Annabel walked to the safe and checked the dial. Still locked.

"I don't think he's bluffing," she said quietly. "He has the key. Or had one. And now he wants to rattle us."

Evie exhaled. "Well, it's working."

Annabel turned to the window, watching Rupert disappear down the lane.

"No. Not yet. But he's worried. That's good."

She looked at Evie. "Now we need to find out exactly what he's hiding — and who's helping him hide it."

Chapter 15

It was well past midnight when Annabel finally reopened the ledger.

The safe creaked slightly as she turned the dial. The pages still carried that old scent — like salt, mildew, and long-held breath. Evie sat cross-legged on the rug with her laptop, searching through online property records and half-forgotten newspaper archives. Persephone was curled beside her like a furry, judgmental bookmark.

Annabel sat at the table, a steaming mug of peppermint tea beside her.

"I keep thinking about what Rupert said," she murmured.

Evie looked up. "The key thing?"

"The 'you've been busy' thing. He didn't just know we'd been to the mill. He *knows* what we found. Or he suspects."

"Maybe both," Evie said. "He's playing chess while everyone else is still looking for the board."

Annabel flipped through the ledger again. The handwriting had grown tighter in the later pages — more anxious, more aware of time running out.

Then she stopped.

A name.

"G.H." – payment for concealment, Crate 11 ledger duplicate removal (1986)

Annabel's brow furrowed. "G.H..."

She reached for Ernie's backup notebook and began flipping pages. In the margin of one of the last entries, scrawled beside a sketch of the mill, Ernie had underlined three initials:

G.H. – knows. Doesn't want it found.

Evie leaned over. "That's not Graham Hargreaves, is it?"

"It has to be." Annabel whispered. "He *was* the one who found the coin. And he gave it to me — but what if that was *after* he tried to get rid of the rest?"

"But... he disappeared," Evie said. "Left us the note. Why would he help and then vanish?"

Annabel turned to the napkin again — the one Bea had given them at the fair.

They know I gave it to her... I should have burned it...

"He was scared," Annabel said. "He knew something. Maybe more than he admitted. And someone didn't want him talking."

Evie stared at the ledger entry.

"He was paid to *remove* a copy of the ledger. In 1986. That means someone —

maybe the second ledger keeper — had duplicated it. And someone like Rupert's father or uncle paid Graham to find and destroy it."

"But Graham didn't destroy *this* copy," Annabel said. "So, either he failed, or... he lied."

***

Silence thickened in the room.

Then Persephone stood up.

She paced once across the rug, then leapt onto the table, staring pointedly at the ledger — and then toward the door.

Evie tilted her head. "Is she suggesting someone else is coming?"

Annabel smiled faintly. "No. She's saying we have what someone wants. And they know where to find us."

***

Annabel reached for a fresh sheet of paper and began drawing columns.

The original wreck

The payments

The second ledger keeper

Graham

The missing duplicate

Rupert

Evie leaned over. "What are you doing?"

"Organising the truth," Annabel said. "Before someone tries to destroy it again."

Persephone jumped down from the table and began pawing at the cupboard under the bookshelf.

Evie raised an eyebrow. "What's she doing now?"

Annabel followed her.

Behind the cupboard, something was taped to the back panel.

A folded letter.

Annabel peeled it off.

She opened it slowly.

***

To whoever finds the ledger:

I tried to keep it safe. But they found out. If this letter's still here, it means I didn't make it back.

Don't trust the ones smiling. Don't trust the ones who remember the wreck fondly.

It wasn't gold that cursed us. It was silence.

— G.H.

***

Annabel whispered, "He *did* leave something."

Evie stared. "That's his final word."

And Persephone?

She sat perfectly still.

As if she had always known where the truth was hiding.

Chapter 16

It was just after dawn when Evie showed up at Honeystone Cottage with a roll of butcher paper, a tangled ball of red yarn, and three thumbtacks already stuck in her sleeve.

Annabel blinked at her from the front door, still in her robe.

"I brought caffeine," Evie announced, holding up a large thermos. "And *justice string.*"

Persephone trotted in behind her, tail high, like this was all perfectly normal.

***

The dining room became the war room.

Annabel cleared the table. Evie unrolled the butcher paper across the back wall. Persephone, after an initial investigation of the string, decided the windowsill gave a superior vantage point and settled in.

Annabel pinned the copy of the fridge photo at the centre.

"Start here," she said. "The knowns."

Evie pinned up names and connections around it:

Rupert Hale — estate agent, key to Annabel's cottage, descendant of Elias Hale

Kitty Simmons — missing from the fair, family name in the ledger

Felix Barlow — public sceptic, family history in the ledger

Mrs. Penfold — suspicious withdrawal from social life

Bea Simmons — gave them Graham's note

Graham Hargreaves — vanished, former cleaner of ledger copies

Maggie Cooke — unconscious, tried to warn Annabel, knew Ernie

Annabel stepped back. "They're all linked to the original cover-up — or trying to clean up what's left of it."

Evie tied red yarn between Rupert and Maggie. "She said 'he was watching Ernie.' We assumed it was Felix, but..."

***

Persephone leapt down from the windowsill.

She trotted over to the yarn — eyed it like prey — and swatted a loop loose from the wall.

It danced through the air, uncoiled... and landed between Kitty Simmons and Rupert Hale. The yarn stuck to both tacks.

Annabel tilted her head.

Evie rolled her eyes. "Really?"

Then she blinked. "Wait."

"She sells her flowers from a greenhouse on Hale property," Annabel murmured.

Evie's eyes narrowed. "And she's always said she gets a 'deal' on the lease. She's always defended him — *always.*"

Annabel stepped forward. "He's protecting her livelihood. She's protecting his reputation."

Evie grabbed a pen and scrawled a thick red arrow between their names.

Persephone sat down beside the accidental link, proud.

Annabel raised a brow. "She's more effective than the village rumour mill."

"She *is* the rumour mill," Evie muttered.

***

They moved on to pinning up the backup notebook, the ledger, and Graham's final letter.

Evie stared at the web.

"I think we've got enough to push someone to snap."

Annabel nodded. "So, we need a trap."

Evie's eyes sparkled. "Oh, I *love* traps."

***

The plan formed slowly, layer by layer:

They would "discover" another clue — one the killer would not know existed. Something that could suggest *a copy of the ledger had already been sent to someone else.*

A message — vague, but damning.

They would say they were going to deliver it to the police the next night.

In person.

At the old chapel where the WI were holding their charity quiz night.

"It has to be public," Annabel said. "Somewhere they'll try to stop us before we arrive. If they take the bait..."

"They'll move," Evie finished. "And we'll be ready."

That night, Annabel stood in the hallway, staring at the red web stretching across her wall.

This had started with a body on a cliff. A notebook in a bush. A cat with opinions.

Now?

It was a war of silence and secrets — and they were about to make it loud.

Persephone leapt onto the sideboard and meowed once.

Permission granted.

Chapter 17

The storm did not wait for subtlety.

By the time dusk fell on Little Firling, the sky had turned a bruised grey, and the first crack of thunder rolled across the village like a warning shot. Windows shuttered. Shop signs swung wildly on their hinges. The sea crashed against the cliffs in great, furious sighs.

Inside Honeystone Cottage, the atmosphere was electric — and not just because the overhead lights had flickered twice.

Annabel paced. Evie watched from the sofa, one eye on her friend, one on

Persephone, who had stationed herself like a gargoyle on the windowsill, tail twitching with quiet aggression.

"Letter is in the envelope," Evie said, holding it up. "No names, no details — just enough to suggest someone else has the ledger and is sending it to the police."

Annabel nodded. "And we'll carry it in plain sight tomorrow night. At the chapel. Public. Loud."

"If someone makes a move tonight," Evie added, "it means they couldn't wait. It means they're desperate."

Thunder rolled again.

Annabel checked the back door. Locked. Then checked it again.

"Do you think it's Rupert?" Evie asked. "Or Kitty?"

Annabel hesitated. "I think it's whoever has the most to lose if this gets out. Maybe not even the killer. Maybe just the clean-up crew."

A beat of silence passed. Then —

Tap. Tap. Tap.

Not at the door.

At the kitchen window.

Both women froze.

Persephone hissed.

Annabel moved toward the window, slowly, heart thudding. Evie followed, her hand already gripping the nearest umbrella like a makeshift weapon.

The porch light flickered on.

There was a figure standing just at the edge of the garden.

Drenched.

Face hidden beneath a hood.

Still.

Watching.

Then — gone. Slipped back into the darkness like smoke.

Evie muttered, "Well, that's not terrifying."

Annabel reached for her phone. "I'm calling Oakes."

***

Ten minutes later, PC Oakes stood in the hallway, boots dripping and expression taut. "You say they didn't knock?" he asked.

"They just watched," Annabel said. "Long enough for us to notice."

Persephone paced around his feet once, then retreated to her post.

"Have you had any other visitors?" he asked.

"Only Rupert yesterday," Annabel said, tone cool.

Evie crossed her arms. "He made a point of reminding us he has a key to the house."

Oakes frowned. "That's not supposed to be true."

"It was true enough," Annabel said. "I changed the locks this morning."

Oakes nodded. "Good. Still—don't go anywhere alone. Either of you."

"What about Maggie?" Annabel asked. "Any change?"

His expression tightened. "Still unconscious. But stable."

"And Graham?" Evie said quietly.

Oakes shook his head. "No sign. Officially listed as missing now."

He glanced around the cottage, then looked at Annabel.

"Whatever you're stirring up — it's working."

Then he left.

***

The rain lashed the windows. The air was thick with waiting.

Persephone jumped into Annabel's lap, curled tightly, and did not purr. Just stared at the door.

"You think they'll come tonight?" Evie asked.

Annabel did not answer.

She just looked toward the darkened hall... and whispered,

"I think they already did."

Chapter 18

The cottage was too quiet.

Even with the storm hurling itself at the windows, the walls of Honeystone held a hush that felt... unnatural. Like the house itself was listening.

Persephone had not moved in twenty minutes.

She sat, coiled on the sideboard, ears forward, tail twitching once every fifteen seconds — the feline equivalent of a ticking clock.

Annabel sat in her armchair; cup of tea untouched. Evie stood near the front door, baseball bat in hand, thumb running slowly along the tape-wrapped handle.

"Midnight is in twenty minutes," Evie muttered.

Annabel did not look up. "If they're going to try to stop us, it'll be now. Before the end of the quiz night. Before we're surrounded by witnesses."

Thunder rolled overhead.

And then — footsteps.

Soft. Outside. Gravel crunching under careful weight.

Persephone's tail froze mid-flick.

Evie tightened her grip on the bat.

A knock. Not polite. Not casual.

Urgent.

Then a voice, muffled through the door. Familiar.

"Annabel. Please. Let me in."

Kitty Simmons.

***

Evie glanced at Annabel, who nodded slowly and moved toward the door.

She opened it just enough to see Kitty — soaked, eyes wide, hair flattened to her forehead. No umbrella. No coat. Just a damp jumper and muddy boots.

"You shouldn't be here," Annabel said flatly.

Kitty stepped forward. "I had to come. I saw someone watching your house. I think they broke into the bakery last night looking for something. I... I think they're after me too."

Annabel hesitated. Evie did not.

"She's lying," Evie said.

Kitty turned, affronted. "Excuse me?"

Evie stepped forward; bat still lowered. "You didn't come to warn us. You came to find out if we had it."

Kitty blinked. "Had what?"

Annabel's voice was soft but firm. "The ledger."

Kitty went still.

Lightning cracked. The room lit up like a photograph. And in that flicker of light, the truth showed on her face.

A mix of fear... and guilt.

Annabel stepped back. "Come in."

***

Kitty entered like a woman stepping onto a stage she did not want to be on.

Evie shut the door behind her and leaned against it. Not blocking the exit. But not *not* blocking it either.

Annabel folded her arms.

"How long have you been working with Rupert?"

Kitty looked up. "I'm not working with him. I never—"

"Kitty," Annabel cut in. "We know about the lease. We know about the land. We know your grandmother's name is in the ledger."

Kitty sat. Hard.

"It was supposed to be over," she said. "He promised. He said it was just history. That if we didn't stir it, it would stay buried."

Evie scoffed. "You mean he told you to keep quiet while he controlled the whole village?"

Kitty's voice cracked. "I didn't know he'd kill anyone."

Silence.

Annabel leaned in. "Who?"

Kitty's lips parted.

Then — *BANG.*

The back door.

Not knocked.

Kicked.

***

Evie moved fast, positioning herself between Kitty and the kitchen. Annabel darted toward the bookshelf — and the safe behind it.

Persephone hissed, loud and low, fur bristling.

The kitchen door burst open.

Rupert Hale stood there.

Soaked. Furious. And not smiling anymore.

"Where is it?" he snapped.

"Too late," Annabel said. "It's already with the police."

A lie. But he did not know that.

His eyes flicked toward the safe.

And Evie stepped between them, raising the bat.

Rupert stopped.

"You've made this messy," he said, breathing hard. "This village could have stayed beautiful. Quiet. *Safe.*"

"No," Annabel said, voice cold. "It would've stayed *rotten.*"

Rupert lunged.

Evie swung.

CRACK.

The bat met shoulder — not hard enough to break, but enough to knock him sideways.

Kitty screamed. Persephone leapt from the sideboard and landed on the kitchen counter like a black bolt.

Rupert stumbled — then froze.

PC Oakes stood in the doorway.

Torchlight in one hand.

Handcuffs in the other.

"You've got a funny idea of safe," he said.

Chapter 19

The storm passed with the dawn.

By the time the clouds broke and pale light touched the rooftops of Little Firling, Rupert Hale was sitting in the back of a police car, soaked to the bone and staring at nothing.

Inside Honeystone Cottage, silence returned — this time not heavy, but *earned.*

Persephone had claimed her usual perch on the arm of the sofa, licking her paw like the events of the night were a mild inconvenience she had personally resolved.

Evie was asleep in the armchair, blanket tangled around her, the baseball bat resting nearby like an old friend.

Annabel stood at the window, tea in hand, watching the lane.

It was over.

***

Two days later, the village was back to pretending everything was normal. Sort of.

Graham Hargreaves had been found.

Injured. Frightened. Hiding in the disused fisherman's hut near the cove. He had panicked after handing over the coin, realizing he had been followed. The blow to the back of his head had come before he could get to Oakes.

He remembered everything now — the payment to destroy the ledger copy, his second thoughts, and the guilt he had carried ever since.

He was recovering in hospital. Quiet. But safe.

Maggie Cooke had woken up that morning.

Her voice was hoarse. Her memory was patchy. But she had squeezed Annabel's hand and whispered:

"He didn't want the gold... he wanted the control."

✳✳✳

Kitty Simmons was avoiding everyone.

Her greenhouse was closed. The herb bundles had withered. But the whispers had not.

Mrs. Penfold returned to her reading group with a fresh batch of lemon shortbread and no mention of her recent "migraine."

Bea Simmons was seen having a long talk with Oakes outside the bakery.

And Tobias Marsh sat on the quay, telling the whole thing to anyone who would listen — now finally vindicated after fifty years of being "that old man with stories."

At the Hare & Hound, Henry the barkeep poured Annabel her usual and set a small saucer of sardine pâté on the bar without being asked.

"For the lady," he said, nodding to Persephone, who had taken up station on the stool beside her.

"She's earned it," Annabel said.

"She always does," Henry replied.

That night, at the cottage, Annabel lit a single candle and set the ledger — now returned from Oakes, sealed in plastic evidence sleeves — inside a wooden box marked *"Michael's Research"* nestling it between old folders he had once used to track the poetry of naval life. He would've found the whole affair fascinating — the betrayals, the gold, the silence. *"Just until I know what to do with you,"* she murmured, pressing the lid closed. *"Michael, keep an eye on it for me, won't you?"*

Evie leaned in the doorway. "What now?"

Annabel smiled.

"I think we breathe. And I think we garden. And if the village wants to whisper about me, let them."

Evie chuckled. "They already do. You're the woman who solved a murder with a cat and a notebook."

Annabel raised her cup. "Not a bad epitaph."

Persephone meowed once, softly, from the window.

Outside, the moon rose.

And Little Firling slept.

Every fair has its secrets.
Little Firling has a body.
Murder Blooms at the Fair
A Little Firling Mystery - Book Two
Belinda Chavremootoo

"In the hush between turning pages, Persephone knows where the truth hides."

Table of Contents

Prologue 1

Chapter 1 2

Chapter 2 16

Chapter 3 28

Chapter 4 40

Chapter 5 47

Chapter 6...55

Chapter 7...62

Chapter 8...68

Chapter 9...75

Chapter 10 81

Chapter 11 90

Chapter 12 97

Chapter 13 104

Chapter 14 110

Chapter 15 117

Chapter 16 125

Chapter 17 131

Chapter 18 137

Chapter 19 145

Epilogue 150

Prologue

The first murder came with a sea mist and ended with a pair of muddy boots and a bottle of elderflower cordial. Little Firling had never quite recovered — not from the body, nor from the way retired literature teacher Annabel Lennox Deighton and her slightly psychic cat Persephone unravelled the truth with garden tools, sharp intuition, and an alarming tolerance for nosy questions.

Now, spring has come again. The snowdrops are blooming, the fair is unfurling, and once more, not everything is as sweet as the jam tent.

Chapter 1

It was the kind of spring morning that made everything seem quietly possible.

The sea mist still lingered over Little Firling, softening the hedgerows and the slate roofs, as if the village had been drawn in pencil, then brushed with water. In the back garden of Honeystone Cottage, snowdrops nodded modestly, their white heads drooping like shy guests arriving too early to a party. Nearby, a scatter of hellebores peeked out, blush-toned and slightly dishevelled, thriving in the chilly earth like they'd been here longer than the cottage itself.

Annabel Lennox Deighton knelt beside a patch of rosemary, adjusting its uneven stems with delicate precision. She wore her old gardening jumper — the one with the elbow patches and faint turmeric stains from a Moroccan stew experiment — and a wool headband that Persephone, her sleek Bombay cat, had tried to steal twice already.

Above her, the New Dawn climbing rose had begun its early stretch — burgundy-tipped leaves unfurling like a prelude to a summer symphony that hadn't quite composed itself yet.

"Ambitious," Annabel murmured, eyeing the new shoots. "Especially considering we had a frost last Tuesday."

Persephone, perched high on the garden wall like a feline gargoyle, gave no opinion. Her glossy black fur shimmered in the pale light as she narrowed her golden eyes at a squirrel attempting acrobatics on the bird feeder.

Annabel smiled faintly. "At least someone around here is focused."

She straightened with a soft groan and surveyed her kingdom — a slightly chaotic Eden with dreams of grandeur.

This year, she had plans.

The Desdemona rose — with its peach-blushed petals and a scent like poetry and apricots — would go by the kitchen door. The Double Delight hybrid tea rose, scandalously beautiful with crimson-tipped petals fading to creamy centres, was destined for the gate. And if she could track down a healthy specimen of Madame Hardy, with her pure white blooms and green eye? She'd give it the best spot in the sun.

And the herb patch?

Also due for an upgrade.

She'd been flirting with the idea of Vietnamese coriander, maybe even shiso, if she could convince the local nursery that she wasn't trying to cultivate "exotic weeds." Bronze fennel, lemongrass, perhaps even a few kaffir lime leaves in a pot, just for show. The kinds of things that made her fingers itch to reach for a pestle and mortar.

Her late husband, Michael, used to tease her — *"You collect herbs the way some people collect stamps, darling."*

But he always cleaned his plate.

Those years they spent travelling — narrow street markets in Istanbul, flower carts in Morocco, a guesthouse in Kerala where a woman taught her to make seven kinds of chutney — those flavours still lived in her muscle memory. Her cooking now was a strange fusion of memory and mood.

She wanted her garden to reflect that. More than neat rows. More than polite blooms.

She wanted wildness. Fragrance. Food. Colour. Drama.

Maybe a little too much.

But then again — maybe not enough.

***

By late morning, the village green was in full, unapologetic bloom.

Bunting fluttered overhead, zig-zagging across the stalls like wild ribbon, while the smell of scones, damp grass, and potting soil mixed into something unmistakably English and mildly chaotic.

The Little Firling Annual Garden Fair had drawn a lively crowd — tweed jackets and floral dresses, toddlers with painted faces, labradors in bandanas, and more than one person cradling a prize pumpkin like it was a newborn.

Annabel adjusted the strap of her shoulder bag and surveyed the scene as if preparing for battle.

"Remind me," she said flatly, "how I agreed to be here again?"

Beside her, Evie Barnes, her neighbour and best friend, sipped from a suspiciously floral thermos. "Because you love plants, you're competitive, and deep down, you enjoy village gossip as much as I do."

"That's a lie."

"It's an *accurate* lie."

Persephone, proudly trotting ahead on her red harness (fashionable and deeply resented), paused every few steps to receive praise, attention, and the occasional smoked salmon treat from passersby.

"She's more famous than I am," Annabel muttered.

Evie didn't look up. "She has better cheekbones."

***

The fair spooled out in every direction:

A plant swap stall, where three pensioners were quietly arguing over a mislabelled lupin.

A tea tent with a long queue and a silver urn wheezing like it was doing overtime.

A table full of handmade soaps named things like *'Basil Meditation'* and *'Joy of Geranium.'*

And at the centre of it all, the main stage, where Dr. Alistair Forsyth stood talking with the village council chair and sipping from his familiar porcelain cup.

He looked exactly how a village doctor should — calm, tidy, and vaguely paternal. But something in Annabel's spine prickled.

"Under five minutes," Evie said. "Place your bets on how long before the first scandal."

Annabel opened her mouth to retort — and the fair delivered.

***

A shout rose from the competitive bloom tent.

Florence Cattermole, formidable in florals, was mid-glare at Ivy Gresham, who stood coolly behind her herb stall in a linen wrap dress and earrings that clinked like windchimes of passive aggression.

"You're selling lies in bottles, Ivy," Florence said crisply. "And calling it medicine."

"And you're selling bitterness in Tupperware," Ivy replied, "and calling it chutney."

Several villagers audibly gasped. Someone dropped a bag of potting mix.

"Ladies," said the jam judge nervously, "please. Not in front of the marigolds."

Florence sniffed, shot a look at Persephone — who blinked imperiously — and swept away in a huff that smelled vaguely of verbena.

Evie murmured, "Ivy wins that round."

Near the tea tent, Henry Radcliffe, cane in one hand, fury in the other, was gesturing wildly at a sign-up sheet for a "Wellness Walk."

"Oh, he's got the nerve to promote *health*? The man gave me the wrong diagnosis and a ruined spine."

His voice echoed across the fairground, silencing a nearby recorder solo.

Margaret Coombes, trying desperately to stay neutral, put a hand on his arm.

"Henry, not now—"

"When then? After another one of his smug speeches?"

Annabel caught Evie's eye. "Second scandal. That's two in five minutes."

"The villagers are warming up," Evie whispered. "By the time we get to the prize tomato, someone's going to throw a fork."

✳✳✳

Meanwhile, Colin Denby, wearing his usual field coat and thousand-yard stare, was standing unusually still near the bee display. He bent slightly toward Persephone, who had stationed herself beside a lemon balm plant like she owned it.

"You feel it too, don't you?" he muttered, eyes darting. "Something's off this year. Things growing where they shouldn't. People saying too much."

Persephone licked her paw.

Annabel raised an eyebrow. "Do we think he talks to every cat like that?"

Evie sipped her tea. "Only the sentient ones."

***

Just as the tension reached a polite simmer, the microphone crackled.

Dr. Forsyth took the stage, notes in one hand, teacup in the other.

"Ladies and gentlemen," he said with a smile. "Thank you all for coming to this year's Little Firling Garden Fair..."

Annabel's tea paused halfway to her lips.

Persephone turned to face the stage, tail flicking once.

Evie leaned over. "That's three. Something's coming."

"Under five minutes," Annabel whispered.

Chapter 2

It happened so quickly, at first no one moved.

Dr. Alistair Forsyth was halfway through thanking the volunteers from the Firling Allotment Society when he paused — a faint, odd twitch in his left shoulder. Then he coughed. Twice. A strange, hollow sound that echoed awkwardly over the microphone.

He reached for the lectern.

Then his cup slipped from his hand and fell, shattering on the stage in a porcelain burst that made a woman near the jam tent yelp.

For a breath, it seemed like nothing more than a slip — a simple stumble, a clumsy moment in the middle of a speech no one was particularly listening to.

But then he collapsed, crumpling like a snapped tulip stem.

Flat on his back.

Still.

***

Gasps rolled through the crowd. A child screamed. Someone dropped a tray of meringues.

Evie stiffened beside Annabel. "Bloody hell."

Annabel was already moving. Her instincts — honed from the last murder that had disrupted their quiet lives — prickled like static.

She reached the stage just as Margaret Coombes shoved her way up, her eyes wide and stricken. "Alistair? Oh, God—Alistair?"

But she didn't touch him.

Because even she could see — he was gone.

Annabel crouched, two fingers at the side of the neck, searching for a pulse she knew wouldn't be there. His skin was already cooling. A faint ring of foam clung to the edge of his lip. His eyes, open and clouded, stared at nothing at all.

She gently closed them.

***

Behind her, voices began rising like a kettle nearing boil.

"What's happened?"

"Is it a stroke?"

"Call Dr. Graves!"

"No, he's not here—he's at the racetrack with—"

"Did he eat the chicken salad?! I *told* them not to put that in the sun—"

Annabel tuned them out. Instead, she looked at the small, shattered teacup beside Forsyth's hand. A few drops of tea still shimmered on the stage floor.

Then she felt it.

A gentle nudge.

Persephone had leapt up beside her, sleek and utterly focused, sniffing the air with her ears back.

She gave a low growl — a soft, uncanny sound — then slowly, pointedly, sat beside the broken cup.

*****

Evie arrived seconds later, breathless. "Is he—?"

Annabel nodded once.

Evie exhaled through her teeth. "You don't think...?"

"I don't know what I think. Yet."

*****

A commotion at the back of the crowd turned every head.

Barrelling toward the stage in a too-large tweed coat and half-laced boots came a man in his early fifties, hair flopping wildly, sunglasses perched like an afterthought atop his head.

He stopped short when he saw the still figure.

"Oh God. Oh *God.*"

Graham Forsyth.

Alistair's brother.

And, as rumour had it, his biggest regret.

***

Margaret's voice sliced through the silence. "Where have *you* been?"

Graham looked at her, red-eyed. "I—I didn't know he was—he was *fine.* We spoke yesterday."

"You stink of beer," she snapped. "He asked you not to come today."

"I just—I thought I'd surprise him—"

Evie muttered under her breath, "Well. Mission accomplished."

Annabel glanced between them. The grief looked real... but then again, grief often did.

***

The fair had dissolved into buzzing speculation. A few villagers were crying. Some were shouting. Florence Cattermole was already organizing a crowd control plan near the tea tent. Someone had brought over a gingham blanket to cover the body, but Annabel insisted it stay untouched.

"This is a crime scene now," she said softly.

Graham's head whipped toward her. "What?! What do you mean crime scene? It was a heart attack, right? I mean—Alistair had... had *blood pressure problems*, didn't he?"

Margaret flinched.

Annabel's gaze narrowed. "Did he?"

There was a beat.

Then Margaret said, very quietly, "Not anymore."

***

A few minutes later, Sasha Eldridge appeared at the edge of the crowd, breathless and pale. "Should we call the new doctor? Dr. Graves?"

Evie raised a brow. "Wasn't he invited to the fair?"

Sasha fidgeted. "He said he doesn't really… do events. Likes to keep to himself."

Margaret gave a sharp sniff. "At least he's *consistent.* Unlike Graham."

Annabel turned. "What do you mean?"

Margaret's mouth tightened. "He was meant to be at the races. Alistair told him *specifically* not to come today."

And right on cue, Graham Forsyth barged through the milling crowd — flushed, eyes wide, his coat caught halfway on, and reeking unmistakably of ale and panic.

"What happened?!"

Margaret turned on him like a blade. "Where were you?!"

Graham stammered. "I—I didn't know. He was *fine* yesterday. We spoke!"

"You weren't supposed to be here."

"I came to make things right."

Evie muttered, "Bit late for that."

Before anyone could answer, Persephone let out a low trill — not quite a meow, not quite a growl — as she stared fixedly at Sasha. Sasha backed a step. "What? It wasn't me!"

Persephone blinked slowly. Like she wasn't *convinced.*

***

A few minutes later, PC Tom Oakes showed up — flustered and out of breath, likely pulled off whatever low-stakes bicycle theft had been his only task today.

Margaret explained everything quickly, in a brittle voice.

Tom scratched his head. "So... it might be poison?"

Annabel looked toward the teacup.

"I think," she said, "we need to keep that cup."

"And the thermos," added Evie.

"And *everyone who touched anything near him*," Annabel finished.

Tom sighed. "We'll have to ask some... questions."

Graham let out a strangled sound. "You're not suggesting I had something to do with this—"

"No one's suggesting anything," Annabel said gently. "But Alistair's not going to explain what happened. So, someone else will have to."

***

Later, as the crowd slowly dispersed, Persephone perched on the edge of the stage, watching the last of the fair's banners flutter in the breeze.

A white petal from the rose tent floated past her.

She didn't look away.

Chapter 3

The Hare & Hound smelled of woodsmoke, damp wool, and suspiciously citrusy floor cleaner — all of which Annabel found oddly comforting.

The fireplace crackled. The lamps were lit. And the usual crowd was buzzing like bees that had accidentally found the gin tent.

Evie pushed open the door like a woman on a mission. "Back corner. Less chance of being cornered by Mrs. Pellham and her theories about alien crop circles."

Annabel followed, shrugging off her coat. Persephone padded in ahead of them, tail high, as if she *owned* the pub. Which, to be fair, most of the regulars would agree with.

Henry Griggs, the barkeep, gave her a respectful nod. "Evening, Miss Persephone."

To Annabel: "Sardine pâtés on the house, yeah?"

"Only if she doesn't judge your trousers," Evie said.

Henry grinned. "She already did."

***

They settled into the corner booth, drinks in hand — red wine for Annabel, something mysterious and bubbling for Evie. Persephone curled up regally beside a dish of pâté and a coaster, like a small god waiting for worshippers.

"Right," Evie said, flipping open her notebook. "Where do we begin?"

Annabel glanced around. The pub was already buzzing.

TABLE ONE: Florence Cattermole holding court

"...and I *told* them, didn't I? I said that man was arrogant. Wouldn't even join the WI quiz night. What kind of monster hates trivia?"

Someone murmured agreement.

TABLE TWO: Sasha with suspicious energy

She was hunched over her cider, whispering fiercely to a man Annabel didn't recognize — maybe someone from the pharmacy? Every few minutes she glanced toward the bar like she was expecting someone. Or avoiding them.

TABLE THREE: Colin Denby... muttering

Of course. He had a notepad. A pint. And an audience of one — an uninterested spaniel.

"I said it was coming. Didn't I say it? Everything grows rotten when you bury truth too deep."

The spaniel farted and walked away.

***

Evie leaned in. "Okay, theory time. Top suspect?"

Annabel sipped her wine. "Too soon. But... Margaret was *very* quick to mention Graham had been told to stay away."

"And Sasha looked like someone who'd mixed the wrong file drawer."

Annabel nodded. "And Ivy Gresham? Was she the only one who didn't look surprised?"

***

Just then, the pub door opened — a blast of cold air, and in stepped a man in a charcoal coat and wire-framed glasses.

Dr. Richard Graves.

New GP.

Quiet. Unsmiling.

Like someone who could perform surgery with a teaspoon and not get flustered.

He nodded at Henry, then spotted Annabel.

And *froze.*

Just for a second.

Then he walked to the bar.

Evie said, "You saw that too?"

Annabel murmured, "He wasn't just surprised to see me. He was surprised to be seen at all."

Persephone opened one eye, stared at Graves for three long seconds... and *growled.*

***

Persephone growled — low and definite — as Dr. Graves turned his back to the room.

Evie arched an eyebrow. "Well. That's never a good sign."

Annabel sipped her wine. "She did once growl at a man who stole a wheelbarrow."

"She also growled at a broccoli floret."

Annabel shrugged. "She's discerning."

Just then, a shadow passed their table — and stopped.

Margaret Coombes, still in her nurse's cardigan and a pale green scarf that didn't quite match, stood holding a half-full glass of white wine and an expression that was trying for calm but missing the mark.

"Mind if I join you?" she asked.

Evie opened her mouth.

Annabel beat her to it. "Of course."

Margaret slid into the bench across from them, placing her wine on a coaster with careful precision.

"I suppose you've heard all sorts by now," she said after a moment.

Evie smirked. "Only three murder theories, two poison suggestions, and one claim that Persephone is psychic."

Persephone blinked once. Superior.

Margaret gave a tight, almost-smile. "Alistair wasn't supposed to speak today. He wasn't feeling well."

Annabel leaned in slightly. "What changed?"

Margaret hesitated. "Graham."

Ah.

Evie folded her arms. "I thought he wasn't even invited."

Margaret swirled her wine but didn't drink. "He said he was going to the races. That he didn't want to 'deal with the villagers.' But Alistair was... tense this week. He wouldn't say why. He just said, 'If he shows up, I want the crowd on my side.'"

Annabel tilted her head. "He thought Graham would confront him publicly?"

"I don't know what he thought," Margaret said. "But he cleaned his office. Removed some old files. He was... preparing for something."

Evie frowned. "Or hiding something?"

Margaret's lips pressed into a line.

Annabel was quiet for a long moment. Then: "Did Graham have a reason to want him gone?"

Margaret looked up sharply. "They were *brothers.*"

"Sometimes that's motive enough."

Margaret's hand curled around her glass.

"They didn't speak for over two years. Not properly. Not since the incident with the Radcliffe case. Alistair took the blame. But it wasn't entirely his fault."

Evie's eyes sharpened. "So, Graham *was* involved."

Margaret didn't answer. But her silence was loud.

***

Persephone flicked her tail.

Across the pub, Graham had arrived — slouched into a stool near the window, ordering something cheap and quick. He looked like a man who wanted to disappear into the floorboards.

Margaret stood abruptly.

"I shouldn't have said anything," she murmured. "But I will say this: if Graham *did* come back to make peace... then fate has a cruel sense of humour."

And with that, she slipped away, leaving behind the faint scent of antiseptic and regret.

***

Evie stared into her drink.

"Tell me again why we thought this year would be quieter?"

Annabel sighed. "Because we're optimists."

Persephone let out a long, theatrical sigh.

Annabel nodded. "Exactly."

Chapter 4

The pub had returned to its usual hum — laughter low, pints clinking, conversations humming like bees in thick hedges. But Annabel's gaze never left the man at the far window.

Graham Forsyth, dishevelled and damp around the edges, was hunched over a pint like it might offer absolution. His shoulders sagged in a way that didn't suggest grief exactly — more like exhaustion. Or dread.

Annabel swirled the last of her wine, watching him.

Evie leaned closer. "He's sweating."

"It's warm in here."

"He's sweating like a man who knows the police are going to find something in his sock drawer."

Annabel gave a tiny smile but didn't look away.

***

Persephone, now curled beneath the table, flicked her tail once. A slow, measured warning.

Evie clocked it immediately. "She knows. She *knows* something."

Annabel whispered, "Or she's just bored and wants us to get a move on."

Evie looked toward the bar. "What do we know about him, really? Beyond what Margaret hinted?"

Annabel straightened slightly. "Let's find out."

***

They approached the bar where Henry Griggs was polishing glasses like they'd personally offended him. He glanced up, saw Annabel coming, and raised an eyebrow.

"Let me guess," he said. "You're not here for a refill."

Evie grinned. "We're here for gossip. Just a dash."

Henry huffed, but not unhappily. "Graham Forsyth? Bit of a ghost, that one. Showed up in town a few times over the years. Alistair didn't much like it."

"What did he do?"

"Whatever he felt like. Mostly losing money at the races. Once tried to sell folk on 'vintage jam' made from expired preserves he bought at a car boot sale."

Evie winced. "Yikes."

Henry leaned in. "But here's the weird bit — he came in last week. Dead sober. Asked me if I thought this place was... ready for change."

Annabel's brow furrowed. "Change?"

"That's what he said. Gave me the creeps. Then he tried to tip Persephone with a chip."

From under the bench, Persephone sneezed. Violently.

*****

Annabel turned to look back at Graham — just in time to see his chair was empty.

She froze.

"Evie."

Evie spun. "No. No-no-no—he was just *there*. I saw him! You saw him!"

"He's gone."

Annabel scanned the pub. No movement. No back door ajar. Just a faint trace of spilled ale on the floorboards and an abandoned coat on the back of the chair.

Graham Forsyth had vanished.

***

Evie swore under her breath.

Persephone emerged from under the bench like a small panther on a mission and trotted toward the back hallway.

Annabel followed.

"Where does that go?" she asked Henry.

"Rear exit. Leads down by the river path."

Annabel didn't wait.

***

Outside, the air was sharp with mist and something sweeter — early blossom on the hedgerows, maybe. The lights from the pub glowed behind them like a stage curtain.

Ahead: no sign of Graham. Just flattened grass by the gate. Footprints? Hard to say in the gloom.

Persephone paused at the path and sniffed the air.

Then, with perfect confidence, she turned left — into the trees.

Evie hesitated. "Are we actually going to follow a cat?"

Annabel adjusted her scarf. "She's never been wrong yet."

Chapter 5

The mist curled low over the path as Annabel and Evie followed Persephone's determined march through the narrow lane that dipped behind the pub and skirted the edge of the riverbank. The air smelled of turned soil, damp moss, and the faint tang of something herbal.

"Do you even know where you're going?" Evie hissed toward the cat.

Persephone didn't dignify her with a glance.

The moon pushed through a gap in the clouds just enough to make out the flattened grass ahead.

Footprints. Fresh.

Annabel leaned forward, peering into the dim. "There. The path splits just beyond the willows."

They rounded the bend—only to stop short.

Because someone was already there.

***

A figure in a long coat, crouched at the base of a hedgerow, gloved hands gently plucking what looked like... wild chamomile?

"Evening," said Ivy Gresham, not looking up. "Bit late for a riverside stroll, isn't it?"

Annabel blinked. "I could say the same."

Ivy straightened slowly, slipping her small shears back into a canvas satchel. "I'm harvesting. Moonlight pulls oils to the surface. Makes the plants more potent."

Evie crossed her arms. "Moonlight and murder in one day. We're all making the most of it."

Ivy tilted her head. "You're looking for someone."

"We're looking for Graham Forsyth," Annabel said, watching Ivy's face. "He slipped out of the Hare & Hound without a goodbye."

"And you think he's out here?"

Persephone meowed in affirmation, brushing past Ivy's boots without breaking stride.

"I saw someone pass this way about ten minutes ago," Ivy admitted, after a pause. "Quick steps. Dark coat. Looked... jittery."

Annabel raised a brow. "You didn't think to mention it?"

"I don't report every man pacing like a guilt-ridden squirrel," Ivy said dryly. "But since you're on the scent... he went left, down the slope. Toward the old boathouse."

Evie narrowed her eyes. "That's where the maintenance shed is, isn't it?"

"And the fishing platform," Annabel added.

Ivy's gaze flicked briefly down the path. "You'd better move quickly."

She turned to go, then paused.

"Annabel?"

"Yes?"

"If you find Graham... ask him what happened *three summers ago.*"

Annabel's brows pulled together. "Three summers ago?" she repeated. "That's a little cryptic, even for you."

Ivy shrugged, but her eyes said more than her tone. "It was quiet. Until it wasn't."

Evie stepped in. "What kind of 'not quiet' are we talking? A fistfight? A scandal? A cover-up involving someone's prize goose?"

Ivy hesitated.

"Let's just say," she said slowly, "Graham disappeared back then too. Only that time, he wasn't the only one."

Annabel blinked. "Someone else disappeared?"

"Not exactly," Ivy murmured. "But someone left. Quickly. And came back different."

"Who?"

Ivy just smiled, but there was no warmth in it.

"It's not my story to tell. But if you want to understand Graham… start there."

Evie was about to fire off another question, but Persephone let out an urgent chirp, tail high, already disappearing down the slope toward the river.

Annabel exhaled. "We'll talk again, Ivy."

"I'll be here," Ivy said. "Plants don't harvest themselves."

She vanished into the mist, the scent of chamomile trailing after her.

****

Annabel stared after her. "Three summers ago?"

Evie shook her head. "I swear, every villager has a timeline and a secret. You need a string board."

Persephone darted ahead with purpose, her tail twitching like punctuation.

Annabel followed.

***

Down by the river, the world narrowed — overgrown hedges, tangled roots, and the glimmer of water slipping past in silence. The old boathouse loomed in the near-dark — just a squat shape against the trees.

No light.

No sound.

Evie whispered, "You think he's in there?"

Annabel didn't answer.

She was already moving.

Chapter 6

The path to the old boathouse was little more than packed earth and memory.

As Annabel and Evie followed Persephone's flicking tail, the trees closed in slightly, the kind of darkness that felt not just *dim* but listening. River mist slid over the ground like breath.

"I don't like this," Evie muttered.

Annabel didn't respond. She was watching the shadows between the reeds. Listening for movement. The quiet was too complete.

The boathouse appeared at the edge of the clearing, slumped against the river like it had grown tired of standing.

One broken shutter flapped loosely.

They crept closer. Persephone stopped just shy of the door and sat.

Annabel whispered, "Do you smell anything?"

Evie sniffed. "Rot. Damp wood. And maybe... onions?"

Annabel pointed. "That's wild garlic."

Evie wrinkled her nose. "How rustic."

Annabel tested the door. Unlatched.

She looked at Evie.

"Let me guess," Evie whispered. "You're going in first?" Annabel pushed it open without a word.

***

The boathouse interior was a box of shadows.

Dust hung in the air. Old fishing gear, a cracked oar, and what looked like a mummified boot lined the walls. There was a narrow wooden bench along one side, and a table covered in a stiff, yellowing cloth.

But no Graham.

"He was supposed to be here," Annabel said softly.

Evie moved to the table, peeled back the cloth—revealing a notebook.

Worn. Leather. Buckled shut with an old ribbon. On the cover, in faded ink: *"A.F."*

Annabel's breath caught. "Alistair Forsyth."

Evie opened it slowly.

Inside: neat, looping handwriting. Medical notes. Lists of symptoms. Pages of treatment plans.

But near the middle — a different kind of entry.

"*Three summers ago — Graham furious. Henry R. refused settlement. Margaret suggested we shred files. Told her no. I won't lie for him again.*"

Annabel and Evie exchanged a look.

Henry R. — Radcliffe.

Graham. Margaret. A settlement?

Annabel closed the book gently.

"We need to leave."

Evie blinked. "You're not going to say we should *take it?*"

Annabel shook her head. "Not yet. Let's make sure we weren't *followed* first."

Persephone hissed softly.

From outside... a crunch.

Of footsteps.

***

Annabel moved to the door and opened it slowly.

No one.

Evie looked around, nerves jangling. "Was that—?"

Annabel nodded. "Someone was watching us."

Persephone, still by the table, now pawed at the floor beneath it.

Annabel knelt, lifted the edge of a broken board — and revealed a small, sealed envelope, aged and brittle.

Inside: a photograph.

Graham and Alistair, standing outside the clinic. Smiling.

Behind them: a woman Annabel didn't recognize.

On the back:

"*Belladonna thrives in shade.*"

***

They left the boathouse with the envelope, the photo, and a thousand new questions.

Persephone led the way, her black tail cutting through the mist like a blade.

Evie exhaled. "So, who is the woman?"

Annabel looked at the photo again.

"I don't know."

But I think she's why someone's killing to bury the past.

Chapter 7

The photo sat on the kitchen table at Honeystone Cottage like a guest who wouldn't explain why she was here.

Annabel, tea in hand, stared at the faded image: Dr. Alistair Forsyth, Graham, and the unknown woman standing just behind them — smiling, slightly out of focus. Her hand rested lightly on Graham's arm, and the look she gave Alistair was... not friendly.

Evie, perched across the table with her boots on a stool, chewed on the end of a pencil. "The handwriting. 'Belladonna thrives in shade.' That's not a label. That's a *warning*."

Annabel nodded slowly. "Or a confession."

Persephone flicked her tail once, the universal sign for *finally, they're catching on.*

✳✳✳

They started where every village mystery should: Florence Cattermole, the WI's iron-fisted historian and tea tyrant, currently gardening beside her Victorian climbing clematis and pretending she hadn't been waiting for visitors all day.

Florence spotted the envelope in Annabel's hand before a single word was spoken.

"I haven't seen that picture in years," she said flatly.

Evie blinked. "You've *seen* it?"

Florence straightened. "Alistair had it on his desk. Tucked behind his calendar. That was... *before it all went wrong.*"

Annabel stepped forward. "Who is she?"

A pause. Then:

"Beatrice Hargreaves."

Evie frowned. "Any relation to—"

"Graham's ex. She used to work at the surgery. Temporary admin. Bright. Ambitious. Didn't take well to being told to 'mind her place.'"

"What happened to her?"

Florence dusted off her gloves, lips tight. "She left. One day she was here, the next— vanished. I heard she went up north. Some say she married a banker. Some say she didn't."

Annabel handed her the photo. "Does the belladonna reference mean anything to you?"

Florence hesitated. "She used to say that. Whenever someone underestimated her. Said it was her 'personal proverb.'"

"*Belladonna thrives in shade. So do I.*"

***

Later, at the cottage, Evie was already halfway through a Google rabbit hole.

"Beatrice Hargreaves, no recent socials. No current address. But guess what?"

She turned the laptop to Annabel.

"There was a Beatrice Hargreaves listed as a witness in a medical ethics hearing. Three summers ago. In Leeds."

Annabel felt the air shift. "Alistair was involved?"

Evie nodded. "As a *silent advisor* on a clinic board. Her testimony? Sealed."

Persephone stretched luxuriously and knocked the photo off the table.

***

Annabel stood, already grabbing her coat. "Time to pay Dr. Graves a visit," she said.

Evie smirked. "Shall I bring snacks?"

Annabel checked her bag. "Bring gloves. Just in case he's growing something poisonous."

Persephone jumped up with a chirp and trotted to the door like, *finally.*

Chapter 8

Dr. Richard Graves's office was pristine.

Annabel noted the arrangement immediately — books alphabetized *by author*, herbs in labelled jars, a single decorative houseplant that looked suspiciously fake.

The kind of space that said *I control everything*.

Graves stood to greet them. Crisp white shirt. Neutral smile. Hands folded like he was always ready for bad news.

"Miss Lennox Deighton. Miss Barnes. And of course... Persephone."

Persephone narrowed her eyes and sat directly in the centre of the rug, staring up at him like she'd already read his soul and found it... untidy.

"Thank you for seeing us," Annabel said smoothly. "We won't take much of your time."

"Of course. I'm always happy to help. Though I must admit," he added with a faint smile, "this seems more like a police matter now."

Evie raised an eyebrow. "And yet you weren't at the fair."

Graves folded his hands. "I've only recently arrived. I felt it best not to insert myself into village activities too quickly."

Annabel tilted her head. "Or perhaps you didn't want to insert yourself before the investigation concluded?"

A flicker of something — just a flash — passed through his eyes.

"I'm not sure I follow."

***

Annabel reached into her bag and placed the photo on the desk.

Alistair. Graham. Beatrice Hargreaves.

Graves didn't react — not with his face. But his fingers twitched once.

"Do you recognize her?" Annabel asked softly.

Graves exhaled. "That was... not part of my role."

Evie leaned in. "What *is* your role exactly?"

He didn't answer.

Persephone stood. Walked to the desk.

Annabel watched her, calmly, as the cat strolled behind Graves's polished chair... stopped at the small side table, and lifted one paw.

A clean, deliberate swipe.

A folder — thick, stamped with a faded "CONFIDENTIAL" seal — slid out from the bottom shelf.

It hit the floor with a soft thud.

Everyone stared at it.

Even Graves.

He didn't move.

Annabel stood, crossed the room, and picked it up.

Internal Review: Dr. Alistair Forsyth – Ongoing

Evie whistled low. "Oops."

***

Graves sat back down.

"I was sent by the board," he said, finally.

"They received multiple complaints over the past three years. About mistreatment. Negligence. Improper disposal of records. One case involved a... misdiagnosis that resulted in permanent injury. Another hinted at coercion. One included your friend, Miss Coombes."

Annabel's jaw tightened. "Margaret?"

"She never formally filed. But she was named... as a witness. Then retracted."

Annabel's voice was sharp. "So instead of a proper investigation, they sent you to poke around quietly?"

Graves looked tired now. "I wasn't meant to confront him. I was meant to observe. To collect. And when the board had enough... they would act."

Evie snapped, "And now he's dead."

Graves nodded slowly. "Yes."

***

Persephone hopped onto the desk like a furry mic drop.

Graves watched her with new respect. Or fear. Possibly both.

"I want that folder," Annabel said. "We'll return it. Eventually."

Graves didn't argue.

***

Outside, the wind had picked up.

Annabel tucked the folder into her coat. "He was hiding a lot."

Evie sighed. "And now we're the ones carrying it."

Persephone trotted ahead, tail high, ears perked — as if she knew the path only got darker from here.

Chapter 9

Back at Honeystone Cottage, the kettle had boiled. The curtains were drawn. Persephone was curled on the windowsill like a velvet punctuation mark.

But the room felt... colder.

Annabel and Evie sat at the table, the thick folder open between them — pages splayed out like fallen leaves, every one of them marked with quiet tragedy.

***

"Three complaints from 2019," Annabel read aloud. "One regarding a missed diagnosis of early-onset diabetes. One where he prescribed the wrong medication entirely. And this one—"

She paused.

Evie leaned in. "Go on."

"A seventeen-year-old girl… misdiagnosed. Sent home. Turned out to be meningitis. She died three days later."

Silence settled between them.

Evie broke it first. "How does a man like that stay in practice?"

Annabel shook her head. "There are excuses listed. Overwork. Staffing shortages. Notes from Graves suggesting that records were *lost*, not hidden. But this—" she tapped a page, voice hardening, "—this shows he altered notes after the fact."

Evie winced. "That's not a mistake. That's a cover-up."

***

Annabel flipped through more pages. "There's a pattern. Some of these patients never filed formal complaints. Others did... and suddenly retracted."

"Or the clinic 'lost the paperwork.'" Evie's voice dripped with disbelief.

They sat back, processing.

***

"The clinic staff must have known something," Annabel said finally.

"Margaret definitely would've. She was his right hand."

"Which means..." Annabel tapped the table, "either she helped protect him... or she was caught in it."

Evie bit her lip. "She's sharp. Observant. She'd notice if her doctor was making bad calls."

Annabel's voice was quiet now. "What if she wasn't just his nurse?"

Evie raised a brow. "You think there was something between them?"

"I think... she had *a reason* to stand by him. Whether it was love, loyalty, fear, or debt... I don't know yet."

Evie opened her mouth, then closed it again.

"Do we confront her?" she asked finally.

Annabel glanced toward the darkening window.

"Not yet."

***

She picked up a smaller slip of paper tucked between the reports. It was handwritten. Not official.

"I know I should've stopped him."
"But I didn't know where the line was anymore."

No signature. But Annabel was willing to bet it wasn't Alistair's handwriting.

***

Persephone leapt down and padded across the table, gently placing a paw on the unsigned note.

Evie blinked. "She's becoming unnervingly good at this."

Annabel smiled faintly, but her eyes stayed on the paper.

"We find out who wrote this. And then we ask Margaret why she let it happen."

Chapter 10

The lights were still on at the Little Firling Clinic, but just barely — one flickering lamp near the front desk, a muted glow from behind the frosted glass of the back office.

Annabel knocked lightly, then pushed the door open.

Sasha Eldridge sat behind the reception desk, hunched over a mug of tea and a half-eaten custard cream. Her blonde bob was slightly frizzy from the rain, and her expression was set to "I'm tired and one sigh away from a nervous breakdown."

When she saw Annabel, she didn't bother with a smile.

"Come to cancel your flu jab?"

Annabel stepped in slowly. "I was hoping to ask you something."

Sasha raised a brow. "I'm off the clock. But if it's not contagious, go ahead."

Annabel held out the folded note — the anonymous confession from Forsyth's file.

"Do you recognize the handwriting?"

Sasha stared at it for a beat too long.

Then she blinked and looked away.

"Nope. Never seen it."

***

Persephone, who had slipped in behind Annabel like the *black silk ghost of truth*, jumped silently onto the reception desk and settled into a sphinx pose.

Sasha glared at her.

"That cat hates me."

Annabel smiled faintly. "She hates liars more."

Sasha scowled but didn't push her off the desk.

***

Annabel took a seat in one of the waiting room chairs. "You were here through most of Dr. Forsyth's career. You must have seen a lot."

Sasha stirred her tea with more aggression than necessary.

"I saw forms. I saw people yelling in the lobby. I saw Margaret crying in the stock cupboard. I saw Alistair pretending not to notice."

That caught Annabel's attention.

"Margaret cried?"

Sasha snorted. "Please. She was devoted to him. Worshipped the ground he walked on — and probably sprinkled antiseptic on it afterward."

"Was it personal?"

Sasha looked up. "He saved her once. Something happened... years ago. She never said what, but after that? She'd have taken a bullet for him."

Annabel considered that. "Or turned one into a syringe."

***

She placed the note gently on the desk again.

"If you didn't write this, who do you think did?"

Sasha hesitated. Then, with a shrug: "Could've been Graham. He used to sneak in here after hours. They fought. Once Alistair threw a clipboard at him. I heard it from the front. Next day, everything was quiet again."

"Why are you still here?" Annabel asked, softly now. "You've seen the files. You know what people are saying."

Sasha let out a long breath and stared into her tea like it held a map to another life.

"Because I don't know how to leave. This place is a mess, but it's *my* mess."

Persephone slowly stretched and flicked her tail into Sasha's tea saucer.

She hissed — not the cat. Sasha.

"Fine. Maybe I've seen that handwriting. Maybe once. On a post-it. Margaret leaves herself reminders in her locker. Stupid little mantras."

Annabel's eyes narrowed. "Mantras?"

Sasha shrugged. "'Do better,' 'don't speak,' 'remember why.' That kind of thing."

Evie, who had been leaning in the doorway the whole time, nodded. "Sounds like a woman trying to hold herself together with hope and denial."

Annabel paused, her hand on the note. "What about... other people? Patients. Families. Did anyone ever come back angry?"

Sasha's eyes flicked to the clock on the wall, like she was debating how much more she wanted to say.

Then she sighed. "There was a woman. Mother of a girl who died — meningitis. Her name was Irene Holt. She came back a year later. Sat in the waiting room every Friday for a month. Said nothing. Just sat."

Evie frowned. "That's... chilling."

"She gave me a tin of biscuits," Sasha said, eyes distant. "Then one day she stopped coming."

Annabel narrowed her gaze. "What happened to her?"

"She lives just outside the village now. On the edge of Firling Cross. Walks with a cane. Her husband—" Sasha lowered her voice "—he blamed Alistair. Fully. Told me once that if karma didn't do the job, he might have to."

Evie made a low whistle. "Well, that's not ominous at *all.*"

Annabel leaned in. "Who else?"

"Bryn Lewis. Claimed Alistair prescribed him a drug cocktail that made his heart worse. Alistair swore it was patient error. Bryn swore it was medical arrogance."

Evie scribbled notes. "And is he the subtle revenge type?"

Sasha snorted. "He once superglued a rude note to the clinic door."

✳✳✳

Annabel stood.

"Thank you."

Sasha gave a tight, wry smile. "If you tell anyone I was helpful, I'll deny it."

Persephone flicked her tail again — this time lightly tapping the edge of the confession note as if to say: *You're getting warmer.*

Chapter 11

The next morning brought mist and low clouds, the kind of sky that threatened rain but hadn't quite committed — perfect weather for secrets.

Annabel and Evie took the long way toward Firling Cross, passing hedgerows heavy with dew and daffodils bowing in silence.

Persephone, despite Annabel's suggestion that she stay warm inside, had simply stared at her, offended, and trotted after them with her usual purposeful grace.

"We're not accusing anyone yet," Annabel said, mostly to herself.

"We're observing," Evie replied. "Like passive-aggressive village wildlife experts."

The cottage of Irene Holt was small, set at the edge of a field lined with hawthorns. Neat lawn. Pristine rose beds. But the curtains stayed closed.

Annabel knocked. They waited. Then the door creaked open a fraction.

Irene Holt looked older than she should have — not in years, but in posture. Her eyes were sharp, her cardigan threadbare at the elbows.

"You're not selling anything, are you?"

Annabel shook her head gently. "We're asking about Dr. Forsyth."

A long pause.

Then: "Dead, is he?"

Evie blinked. "You didn't know?"

"I knew something had shifted. The village goes quieter when someone finally gets what they deserve."

Annabel hesitated. "Do you believe someone did this deliberately?"

Irene's expression didn't change. "I believe justice comes eventually. The method is irrelevant."

Persephone meowed softly.

Irene looked down. "That cat always did like my garden."

"You sat in the clinic lobby. Fridays."

"I did." She opened the door a little wider. "To remind him I hadn't forgotten. To make him look at what he'd done, every week."

"Why did you stop?"

"Because eventually... he stopped looking back."

The door closed.

***

They found Bryn Lewis outside The Hare & Hound, smoking something that probably wasn't legal and aggressively sanding a walking stick.

"Thought you'd be sniffing around soon enough," he grunted.

Annabel nodded. "We heard you had a history with the doctor."

"History? That man put me on a drug that nearly killed me. Then blamed *me* for taking it wrong."

Evie raised an eyebrow. "You seem pretty alive."

"Oh, I'm alive. *He's not.* Convenient, innit?"

Annabel studied him. "Did you ever tell him you'd get revenge?"

Bryn looked up sharply. "I *told everyone.* If karma didn't take him, I'd finish the job."

Evie leaned in. "So... karma's timing saved you the effort?"

He didn't flinch. "Maybe."

Annabel took a step closer. "And now?"

He exhaled. "Now I get to fix up me shed in peace. And no one's knocking asking for bloody wellness brochures."

"But you didn't do it," Annabel said softly.

"Didn't say I didn't," he shot back — and walked away, whistling.

***

Later, back at the cottage, Evie flopped into a chair. "So, Irene's intense and poetic. Bryn's just... mad."

Annabel flipped through the file again.

"Both had motive. But neither had access. Neither knew about the internal review. Neither had tea with him on the day."

Evie nodded slowly. "We've circled the garden beds. And all the footprints lead back..."

"To the surgery," Annabel said. "And to Margaret."

Persephone gave a single, pointed chirp.

"Alright, alright," Evie muttered. "Time to repot some secrets."

Chapter 12

The garden behind Margaret Coombes' cottage was immaculate.

Box hedges trimmed to within an inch of their lives. Lavender pruned to perfect symmetry. Not a single weed dared peek through the gravel path. If control were a place, this would be it.

Annabel, with Evie beside her and Persephone at her heels, knocked once on the back gate.

It opened before she could knock again.

Margaret stood in her gardening gloves, a smear of compost on her cheek, eyes wary.

"If you're here for gossip, I suggest the pub."

Annabel held up the manila folder — Forsyth's internal review — and the folded note with Margaret's unmistakable handwriting.

"We're here for the truth."

***

Inside, the kettle was already hissing, as if Margaret had been expecting them.

She poured the tea with calm hands but tight lips. The mugs were plain. The tension was not.

"You've read the file," she said, more statement than question.

Annabel nodded. "We know there were complaints. Patterns. A system built to hide failure."

Evie added, "And someone who tried — quietly — to stop it."

She slid the note forward.

I know I should've stopped him.

But I didn't know where the line was anymore.

Margaret stared at it.

She didn't deny it.

***

"He saved my life," she said quietly, finally. "Years ago. A cancer scare. He caught it early.

Pushed for tests when no one else believed me. I survived because of him."

A long breath.

"So, when the complaints started... I didn't want to believe them. I thought — people make mistakes. He was overworked. Tired. Maybe they were wrong."

Annabel said nothing.

"But then Graham came back. Angry. Vicious. Dragging up the past. And I saw... *Alistair change.* He started second-guessing himself. Then blaming others. Then... hiding things."

Evie's voice was gentle. "Why didn't you report him?"

"Because I loved him," Margaret whispered. "Not romantically. Not even as a friend. But with that kind of *terrible, desperate loyalty* that makes you blind."

Persephone jumped onto the kitchen counter and knocked over a small ceramic pot.

Inside? A torn scrap of paper.

Margaret flinched.

Annabel retrieved it. A page from a diary?

"Graham won't stop. Beatrice was just the beginning. He'll ruin everything."

Evie's eyes widened. "So, there was something with Beatrice."

Margaret nodded, tears now slipping down her cheek silently.

"They had a relationship. Quiet. Complicated. She left after something went wrong. I never knew the whole story, only that

Graham blamed Alistair. And when she was called to testify… Alistair *panicked.*"

Annabel leaned in. "Did Graham kill him?"

Margaret shook her head.

"I don't know. But I know Graham *wanted to confront him at the fair.* He said… he had something that would end it all."

"And you?" Annabel asked softly. "Did you have something to protect?"

Margaret looked up, broken but unashamed.

"Only what I believed in. Until it shattered."

***

They left in silence.

Persephone paused at the gate, tail flicking once.

Evie murmured, "She's not guilty. But she's not innocent either."

Annabel looked toward the village green.

"Then we'd better find the person who is."

Chapter 13

The Firling Downs Racetrack wasn't glamorous. It smelled of stale ale, damp turf, and fried onions — and the punters ranged from weathered pros in tweed caps to locals squinting at racing slips like they were trying to decode ancient runes.

Annabel, Evie, and Persephone (smuggled in via determined handbag) made their way through the small Saturday crowd toward the food stall near the paddock — where a familiar hunched figure was slumped over a polystyrene tray of chips and gravy.

Graham Forsyth.

***

He looked up before they spoke.

"I figured you'd find me."

Annabel sat beside him on the low brick ledge. "We've got questions."

"I'm not surprised." He took a chip. "You want to know if I killed my brother."

Evie said, "We want to know what you're not telling us."

***

Graham stared out at the track for a long moment.

"I left the village on Friday afternoon," he said. "Took the train. Stayed overnight in Mickleham with an old mate — Freddy Lowes.

He's got CCTV on his front porch, and a timestamped pizza delivery at 8:12 p.m."

Annabel raised an eyebrow. "And the next morning?"

"We didn't leave the house until ten. Watched the early races from his sofa. I've got time-stamped betting receipts from the app. You want them?"

Evie nodded slowly. "So, you couldn't have tampered with the tea."

"Didn't touch his mug, his herbs, his bloody flower collection. Last time I saw Alistair, it was three weeks ago. And yes, we shouted. I wanted him to come clean. But I didn't kill him."

***

Annabel held out the photo.

"Tell me about Beatrice."

Graham flinched.

"He ruined her," he said quietly. "He gaslit her, made her think she was paranoid. She caught him shredding test results. She confronted him."

"What happened?"

"He called her unstable. Got her transferred. Then blackballed her from three clinics."

Evie frowned. "But she testified against him?"

Graham nodded.

"She used a different name. Bea Holloway. After her mother's maiden name. She told the board *everything*. But it was sealed. Quiet settlement. She went off the radar."

Annabel's eyes sharpened. "Until now?"

Graham nodded. "She reached out. Said she was thinking of coming back. She wanted closure. Said she might even talk to a reporter."

"Did Alistair know?"

"I think he *suspected*. He was on edge. Cleaning up files. Panicking."

***

Annabel sat back.

"Do you think someone killed him to protect him?"

Graham laughed — bitter and cracked. "No one ever protected Alistair. Not really. People just let him lie. And sometimes that's worse."

***

They left Graham staring out at the track.

Persephone trotted beside them, silent, thoughtful.

Evie spoke first. "So... he's not our killer."

Annabel sighed. "No. But he might have gotten someone else killed."

Evie blinked. "Beatrice?"

Annabel nodded. "If she was coming back... someone might've wanted to stop her too."

Chapter 14

The clinic was closed for the afternoon. A printed sign on the door read "Staff Training," but Annabel and Evie both knew that was code for Dr. Graves Wants Everyone Gone.

Which made it the perfect time to knock.

Persephone, naturally, slinked in before the door had fully opened.

Dr. Graves didn't look surprised to see them.

"I wondered when you'd come back."

Annabel walked in calmly. "We need more."

He gestured to the chairs across from his desk. The room still smelled faintly of mint and antiseptic — too clean for real peace.

"We've identified Beatrice," Annabel began. "She's using the name Bea Holloway. We know she testified. You had to know that too."

Graves folded his hands. "Her name was redacted in the version you saw. I had the full file."

Evie narrowed her eyes. "And you didn't think to tell us?"

"It wasn't relevant to the board investigation anymore. She disappeared after the hearing. No forwarding contact. No one's seen her in nearly two years."

Annabel leaned in. "Did you look?"

Graves blinked. "No."

"Then you underestimated her. She was planning to return."

That caught him off guard. His posture shifted slightly. "How do you know?"

Evie grinned. "Oh, you know. The way women do — via breadcrumbs, cats, and furious ex-boyfriends."

***

Annabel shifted the tone.

"We want to talk about Alistair's wife. Delia Forsyth. Died two years ago. Reported as natural causes. No autopsy."

A long silence.

"She'd been sick," Graves said finally. "Autoimmune complications."

"Did she trust him?" Annabel asked.

Graves didn't answer.

Evie: "Did *you* trust him?"

Graves hesitated — then stood. Moved to the bookshelf.

From behind a row of journals, he pulled out a sealed envelope, unmarked, thick.

He laid it on the desk.

"This... didn't go in the board report. It was left anonymously in my clinic box a month ago. No name. Just a note that read: '*He's done it before.*'"

Annabel opened the envelope.

Inside were a copy of Delia Forsyth's prescription history, her patient notes (some with worrying gaps) and a note in shaky handwriting: *She didn't want the pills. She stopped taking them. But he kept pushing.*

***

Evie whispered, "Do you think he poisoned her?"

Graves said nothing. But he didn't deny it.

***

"And who else?" Annabel pressed. "You've seen the files. Talked to staff. Who else hated him?"

Graves sat again. "Not everyone hated him. Some feared him. Some depended on him. But…"

He pulled out another paper.

"There was a complaint from a former staff member. A name you might recognize. Maggie Cooke."

Annabel looked up sharply. "The baker?"

"She was," Graves said. "These days she runs the flower shop. Said she needed something quieter."

He paused. "People find their own way to heal, I suppose."

"Used to be a care assistant. Worked with Alistair when he did elder home visits. Filed a concern… then retracted it."

Annabel leaned back. "Why retract it?"

Graves folded the papers away. "He had a way of making people feel small. Stupid. Overreactive. Especially women."

Annabel's voice went quiet. "So, this whole village was trained to excuse him."

Persephone jumped onto the desk, stared Graves down, and gave a low growl.

****

Outside, the clouds were gathering.
Inside, the storm had already begun.

Chapter 15

The scent hit them before the bell did — a heady swirl of lilies, eucalyptus, and something faintly citrus that Evie immediately suspected was "a soap trying too hard."

The window read:

Cooke & Vine – Flowers for Every Season

...in curling gold script Annabel was pretty sure Florence Cattermole hated.

As they stepped inside, Evie muttered, "Last year she was frosting cupcakes and threatening anyone who said her almond tarts were dry."

Annabel smiled. "She was in a coma, Evie. Some people take up journaling. Maggie took up floristry."

Evie shrugged. "Trauma and begonias. Could be worse."

***

Inside, Maggie Cooke was elbow-deep in white roses and dusty miller, tying ribbons with a focus that could've defused a bomb. The shop was warm, filled with soft jazz and barely controlled chaos — glass vases clinked faintly, and someone had overwatered the ferns again.

"If you're here for last-minute peonies in March," Maggie said without looking up, "save us all the drama."

Annabel stepped forward. "Not flowers. Just truth."

✳✳✳

Maggie didn't flinch, but the ribbon in her hand tore.

She straightened slowly, brushing off her apron, eyes landing briefly on Persephone, who had jumped onto the counter and was eyeing a duck-shaped ceramic planter like it owed her money.

"I figured someone would come knocking."

Evie glanced around. "Didn't think it'd be in a flower shop, to be honest. You used to bake."

Maggie gave a tired smirk. "Flour started giving me flashbacks."

Annabel's voice was gentle. "So, you changed course."

"Yeah," Maggie said. "Baking felt loud. Flowers don't scream when things go wrong."

***

Annabel laid the note on the counter.

The shaky handwriting. The weight of implication.

She didn't want the pills. She stopped taking them. But he kept pushing.

"You've seen this before," Annabel said. "Haven't you?"

Maggie nodded.

"Pinned to the back of Delia's medicine cabinet. I found it during a home visit. Didn't think anyone else had noticed."

"You filed a complaint," Annabel said. "Then you retracted it."

"Because the next day, my mum — who needed a prescription urgently — suddenly ended up at the bottom of the patient list. Deliberate or not, Margaret delivered the message with a smile and a 'maybe you misunderstood.'"

Evie winced. "That's calculated."

Maggie looked down. "It was protection. She thought she was keeping everything afloat. Or maybe just keeping *him* afloat."

***

"Did you know Bea Holloway?" Annabel asked.

Maggie flinched, just slightly. "Everyone knew Bea. Smart. Brave. Too good for the place."

"She left?"

"She ran. After she found something. I never knew what — just that it shook her. She said, 'They buried Delia. They'll bury this too.' Then she vanished."

Evie leaned in. "But she told you she was going to the board?"

"Yes. Then I never heard from her again."

***

Persephone chose that moment to knock the duck planter off the counter.

It hit the floor. Shattered.

Maggie didn't flinch.

Evie muttered, "She's so dramatic lately."

Annabel, still watching Maggie, said softly, "And who else might have known what Bea found?"

Maggie took a breath. "Maybe Colin Denby. He used to garden for the Forsyths. He was quiet, but he saw things."

"Like what?"

"Like Delia talking to the birds. Or crying in the rose beds. Like how her prescriptions changed, even when she didn't."

Annabel nodded slowly. "Colin it is, then."

***

They left without another word.

As the door shut behind them, Evie said, "So, Maggie's not a killer."

Annabel looked ahead, thoughtful. "No. But she saw the roots. She just couldn't stop the bloom."

Persephone flicked her tail once — like a full stop on a sentence no one wanted to finish.

Chapter 16

Colin Denby's cottage sat at the far edge of Little Firling, hidden behind a thicket of old hazels and flowering quince. The kind of place most villagers forgot existed — which was exactly how Colin liked it.

Annabel, Evie, and Persephone followed the worn path to his crooked gate, where a carved wooden sign read: "Tread Softly — Roots Remember."

Evie muttered, "That's not creepy at all."

***

Colin answered the door in mud-stained trousers and a jumper that had known better decades. His hair, like the moss on his fence, was unbothered by time or trimming.

"Ladies," he said, blinking slowly. "And Miss Persephone."

The cat, of course, walked in first.

***

His home smelled of dried thyme, old books, and peat. The living room had more plants than chairs. A teapot steamed quietly beside a half-finished puzzle of some ancient ruin overtaken by ivy.

"What brings you to my overgrown corner?" he asked, pouring tea into mismatched mugs.

Annabel held up the photo — Alistair, Graham, and Bea.

"We know she used the name Bea Holloway. We think you knew her."

Colin looked down at the photo, then at Persephone.

"She used to sit right there," he said, pointing to the windowsill. "Said the light made her feel honest."

Evie asked softly, "Did she write to you?"

Colin didn't answer. But Persephone jumped onto a nearby shelf and began batting at a row of old gardening journals.

Thump. One fell to the floor.

Inside: a letter.

***

Annabel opened it.

Handwritten. Folded twice. Dated two weeks before the fair.

Colin,

I've decided. I'm coming back. I can't let him die thinking he won. If I vanish again, let them know I tried.

— Bea

Annabel's voice was steady. "You didn't tell anyone?"

Colin's hands trembled slightly. "She trusted me. Said she needed a week to gather evidence. I didn't want to betray that."

Evie frowned. "Did you tell Alistair she was coming?"

"No. But I think Margaret knew. Somehow. She always knew things she shouldn't."

***

Annabel looked at the letter again. "Why was she so afraid?"

Colin stared into his tea.

"Because she knew what happened to Delia. And she knew Alistair wasn't done hiding things."

A long silence.

"I was supposed to meet her. The morning after the fair. She never showed."

✳✳✳

Outside, the wind picked up.

Inside, Persephone curled beside the cold hearth, eyes half-lidded — like she'd just solved the case and was waiting for everyone else to catch up.

Chapter 17

The Hare & Hound was quieter than usual, but no less nosy.

The bunting from the garden fair still sagged in the corner, a few stray petals scattered on the hearth. A fire burned low, and the gossip burned higher.

Annabel and Evie slid into their usual booth with a quiet nod from Henry Griggs, the bartender, who poured their drinks without asking.

Persephone leapt up beside them, ignored the sardine pâté this time, and instead perched like an interrogator waiting for the next suspect.

"You can feel it," Evie murmured. "Everyone's jumpy."

Annabel nodded. "We just have to let them talk."

TABLE ONE: Florence Cattermole, sharp as ever

"You ask me, Margaret's barely left the house since the fair. Keeps her curtains closed all day. Which is suspicious, *unless she's got something hideous blooming in her garden.*"

Evie whispered, "Or a conscience."

***

TABLE TWO: Sasha Eldridge, hunched over her cider

Sasha sat alone, flipping a beer mat, her knee bouncing.

Henry approached her with a drink. She looked up.

"Thanks," she muttered. "Even though I'm off the rota."

He gave a small smile. "Clinic's not the same without your whispering rage."

Sasha huffed. "It's not rage. It's repressed trauma and caffeine withdrawal."

She paused.

Then added quietly, "You know, he used to mix up prescriptions when Margaret was off. I always corrected them. But if I hadn't... I wonder how many people would've been hurt."

Annabel and Evie shared a look.

"Did you ever report it?" Evie asked.

Sasha glanced around. "No. Because Margaret would say I was overreacting. And she *ran* that place. Not Alistair. Not even the board. It was *her* clinic."

***

TABLE THREE: Colin, surprisingly talkative now

He waved them over with a glass of ginger wine.

"I remembered something," he said softly. "Day of the fair. I saw Margaret early — before it opened. She was headed toward the green, carrying something in a thermos flask."

Annabel blinked. "A thermos?"

"She said it was special tonic. For the 'guest tent.' But she walked past the tent entirely."

Evie leaned in. "Where did she go?"

"Toward the tea stall."

***

Silence. Weighty. Confirming.

Persephone gave a long, slow blink.

***

As they left, Evie whispered, "Sasha corrects Alistair's mistakes, Margaret overrules the staff, and Colin saw her with *the flask.*"

Annabel's jaw tightened. "She didn't just know what Alistair did."

"She tried to stop it being exposed."

Persephone meowed.

"She *killed* to protect a lie."

Chapter 18

The garden behind Margaret Coombes' cottage was still too perfect.

Even the wind couldn't muss the hedges. The lavender stood like soldiers. But today, the flowers didn't comfort — they stared.

Annabel rang the bell.

Evie crossed her arms.

Persephone curled on the stone wall, unblinking.

Margaret opened the door wearing her usual cardigan, her hair pulled into a neat twist. But her eyes looked tired — like she'd been up all-night waiting for this exact moment.

"Come to accuse me, then?"

Annabel didn't blink. "We came for the truth."

Margaret stepped aside.

***

Inside, tea was already steeping.

"Chamomile?" Margaret offered.

Evie looked at the mug like it was ticking. "Hard pass."

They sat at the small table. Margaret took her cup but didn't sip.

***

Annabel placed a folder on the table.

"Sasha told us about the prescription errors. About how you made the clinic run. Not Alistair."

Margaret said nothing.

"Colin saw you the morning of the fair. With a thermos."

Still nothing.

"You told him it was for the guest tent. But you never went there. You went to the tea stall."

Margaret set her cup down. The tiniest tremble in her hand.

Evie leaned forward. "Was it poison? Or medicine he didn't need?"

Margaret closed her eyes.

"It was belladonna."

Silence.

Even the kettle on the hob seemed to pause.

***

"He wasn't supposed to die," Margaret said finally, voice cracked open. "Just sleep through the fair. Miss his speech. Delay the scandal."

Annabel's voice was low. "You wanted to protect him."

"I wanted to protect the *idea* of him," Margaret whispered. "The doctor who saved me. The man who fought the board. Who held it together while everything around him rotted."

She opened her eyes.

"But he changed. After Delia. After Bea. He started silencing everything that threatened him. And when I found out Bea was coming back..."

Annabel finished it for her. "You panicked."

Margaret nodded. "He said he'd handle it. And I believed him. Until I saw the envelope she sent — unopened, in his bin. He never planned to listen. He was going to bury her. Again."

***

Evie spoke. "So, you brewed the tea."

"I put in just enough belladonna to make him groggy. Nothing fatal. I swear it."

Annabel stared at her. "But it was."

Margaret swallowed. "He had a heart condition. One I didn't know about. It... accelerated everything."

"You were his nurse," Evie said. "You should have known."

Margaret looked at her, eyes shining.

"I stopped being his nurse a long time ago. I was just the shadow holding his secrets."

***

Outside, a robin chirped like it didn't know the world had changed.

Persephone hopped off the wall and scratched once at the door. Then sat. Waiting.

"Will you turn me in?" Margaret asked.

Annabel stood.

"You already did."

Margaret's hands were clenched in her lap now, the tea untouched.

"He ruined everything he touched. Not all at once — in small ways. Quiet ones."

Annabel asked softly, "Is that what happened with Bea?"

Margaret nodded. "She wanted to believe the system would work. That the board would listen. But when they didn't... she fell apart. The only person who kept her grounded was Ivy."

Annabel blinked. "Ivy Gresham?"

"They were close. Ivy's the one who told her to leave. Said she'd water her garden until she was strong enough to come back."

Evie narrowed her eyes. "Did Ivy know what you planned?"

Margaret frowned. "No. I never told her."

Annabel went still.

So did Persephone.

A shadow moved outside in the garden of Margaret.

Chapter 19

The sun was pale when they reached Ivy Gresham's cottage — a soft gold filtered through the last of spring's clouds.

Her garden was blooming in quiet chaos.

Yarrow, sage, valerian, feverfew. Things with lovely names and darker uses.

Annabel, Evie, and Persephone stood at the gate.

Ivy was already in the herb beds, snipping something into a wide straw basket.

"Hello," she said without turning. "I thought you'd come."

***

They walked slowly through the rows. The air smelled like lemon balm and wet earth.

Persephone padded along the path, then stopped abruptly — her gaze fixed on a patch of tall green stalks near the back fence.

Foxglove.

Purple. Heavy-headed. Blooming strong.

Annabel stopped beside her. "That's unusual for your garden."

Ivy didn't look up. "Not really. It thrives in shade."

***

Evie's voice was quiet. "Margaret says you were close to Bea."

"I still am. We write."

Annabel stepped forward. "You knew she was coming back."

Ivy clipped a sprig of wormwood. "She'd made up her mind."

"So why didn't you let her finish it?"

That was when Ivy looked up.

Her face was calm. Not guilty. Not defensive. Just... still. "Because she didn't need to."

***

"You slipped the foxglove into the tea," Annabel said.

"I did."

"Why?"

Ivy rose slowly, wiping her hands on her apron.

"Because Margaret's plan wouldn't work. Alistair wouldn't sleep. He'd adapt. He'd spin. He'd crush Bea again, just like before. And she would break all over again."

Evie's voice was hoarse. "So, you killed him for her?"

Ivy looked at them, the wind catching the hem of her dress, the foxglove swaying behind her.

"I killed him for what he'd already done. And for what he would've done again. I knew the dosage. I measured it precisely. It was clean. Quick. Quiet."

Annabel stepped closer. "Bea didn't know."

"Of course not. She's the truth-teller. I'm the weed-puller."

***

Persephone walked to Ivy's feet and sat; tail wrapped like a question mark.

Ivy looked down.

"I don't regret it," she said softly. "You can tell the police, if that's your next step."

Annabel didn't answer right away.

She looked at the foxglove. At the garden. At the woman who saved her friend in the most final way possible.

Then she said: "I think some things thrive in shade because they have no choice."

Epilogue

Spring had shifted to early summer, and Honeystone Cottage was fully awake now — the New Dawn climbing rose halfway up the trellis, Desdemona glowing by the kitchen door, and Double Delight opening like it had just remembered it was the most beautiful thing in the garden.

Annabel knelt in the herb bed, gently tucking a sprig of bronze fennel beside the lemongrass.

"You're dramatic," she murmured to it. "You'll get along with the cat."

Persephone, as if summoned, stretched on the windowsill with theatrical flair and then blinked at a bee like it was beneath her.

∗∗∗

Inside, the kettle was on. Evie was at the table, flipping through the latest issue of *British Gardening for the Slightly Suspicious.*

"So, Margaret's moved to Devon. Retirement by exile?"

Annabel nodded. "She said she wanted to grow sweet peas and not talk to anyone for three years. Reasonable."

"And Bea?"

Annabel smiled. "Bea's staying in the Cotswolds for now. Writing again. Ivy sends her dried herbs in unlabelled brown packets and handwritten notes that could be either recipes or coded warnings."

Evie chuckled. "Therapeutic."

"Potentially criminal," Annabel said, pouring tea. "But very therapeutic."

***

She settled into her chair and glanced toward the window, where the sun was hitting the foxglove just behind the low stone wall.

Yes, she'd planted one.

Just one.

And only in deep shade.

Evie raised an eyebrow at her. "You know, you didn't quote a single author the entire time."

Annabel blinked. "Did I not?"

Persephone gave her a judging look.

Annabel sipped her tea.

"Very well, if it must be remedied… *'In time, we hate that which we often fear.'*"

Evie smirked. "Shakespeare?"

Annabel nodded. "Troilus and Cressida."

"Very brooding of you."

"I'm in my tragic heroine arc. Let me have it."

***

The church bell rang once. Someone trimmed a hedge too enthusiastically down the lane. Somewhere, bees kept working like nothing had happened.

And in the centre of it all, Persephone blinked slowly — as if to say: *until next time.*

Secrets glitter. Truth shatters. And in Little Firling, even heirlooms carry grudges.

Murder beneath the Ballroom Chandelier

A Little Firling Mystery - Book Three

Belinda Chavremootoo

Table of Contents

Prologue 1

Chapter 1 3

Chapter 2 15

Chapter 3 23

Chapter 4 30

Chapter 5 35

Chapter 6..40

Chapter 7..48

Chapter 8..52

Chapter 9..59

Chapter 10..64

Chapter 11..69

Chapter 12..73

Chapter 13..78

Chapter 14..82

Chapter 15..87

Chapter 16..92

Chapter 17..96

Epilogue 107

Prologue

Little Firling had never needed help keeping secrets.

They lived in the stone of the old mill, nestled beneath rose trellises, tucked into second scones at the Hare & Hound pub. And when those secrets grew too heavy to bear, they tended to slip — through misplaced letters, forgotten heirlooms, or the occasional suspicious death.

In her short time living there, Annabel Lennox Deighton, retired literature professor and recent transplant from Glasgow, had already uncovered more mysteries than most villagers experienced in a lifetime. With her sharp mind, a well-worn notebook, and a cat who refused to be left out of anything, she'd solved a death on the cliffs and uncovered long-buried treasure.

But the past never stays buried for long in Little Firling.

Now, spring has brought flowers, festivities... and a gala that will end with a glittering crash.

Because in Little Firling, murder blooms when no one's looking.

And Persephone is always watching.

Chapter 1

It was the kind of evening that dared you to blink.

Lanterns glowed like suspended stars above the gardens of Everly House, and inside, the ballroom shimmered under the weight of a thousand reflections. Gilded mirrors. Polished marble. Sequins. Ambition.

The scent of cut lilies mingled with beeswax polish and something faintly metallic — the smell of money, secrets, and heirlooms that had been fought over in court. Velvet drapes muffled laughter and gossip into a kind of conspiratorial hush, like the walls themselves were in attendance, listening closely.

The strings played soft and slow — the sort of music designed to make you feel wealthy, even if you weren't. The chandeliers twinkled like they were in on a secret. And the champagne? Breathtakingly dry and impossible to hold on an empty stomach.

Annabel Lennox Deighton sipped hers anyway. Annabel had once lectured on Shakespearean tragedy at the University of Glasgow — a career marked by sharp analysis, dry wit, and a faculty nickname that translated roughly to "the velvet scalpel." Retirement hadn't dulled her instincts. If anything, Little Firling's quiet veneer offered new stagecraft for her mind: smaller dramas, tighter scripts, but just as much blood beneath the surface.

She stood near the edge of the ballroom, one eyebrow arched at a topiary that had been shaped, inexplicably, into a swan wearing a powdered wig. A nod to the Versailles theme of the gala, she supposed, though she'd seen fewer wigs and more weaponised gossip.

"If this is meant to be Versailles," she murmured, "they've taken creative liberties."

"Darling," said Evie Barnes, appearing at her elbow, "they're nobles. Creative liberties are a lifestyle."

Evie had been raised in the village — or more precisely, rescued by it. Her aunt, the late Constance Caldwell, had taken her in from the orphanage when she was six and raised her above the village bookshop with stern affection and endless paperbacks. Evie commuted regularly to Surrey to work as a journalist, sharp-eyed and sharper-tongued, before staying after her aunt's passing. She now ran the bookshop — and a running commentary on village life — with dry humour that sometimes masked her wariness. She didn't make friends easily. Annabel had recognised that immediately. And then made herself the exception.

Their invitation had arrived through a combination of favours and horticulture — Annabel had recently helped re-catalogue the Everly House archive for a family legacy exhibit, and the Little Firling Garden Society had contributed to the event's flamboyant theme. It had been meant as a community showcase. The Everly family had turned it into theatre.

Which is how two clever women — and one very particular Bombay cat — ended up drinking champagne beneath a chandelier while surrounded by powdered wigs, faux French accents, and social tension so thick it needed carving knives.

Persephone, of course, had not been invited. She had simply arrived — as she always did when something terrible was about to happen.

At present, she lounged near the base of the dais, watching the room with narrowed eyes and that particularly regal contempt reserved for murder suspects and people who used synthetic lavender.

Annabel hadn't taken the archival work out of boredom — not quite.

It had begun with a polite letter from Lady Vera, a nudge from the Garden Society, and maybe a whispered memory of her late husband, Michael, lingering in the corners of her old study.

She hadn't been looking for work.

But after decades of teaching, her mind still paced like it needed something to solve. Vera's invitation had come with flattery and veiled expectations — "You're sharp, Deighton. You see through things. I need that."

The job hadn't paid, not in anything that mattered.

But it gave her keys to the Everly library.

Access to Vera's "legacy drawers."

And perhaps, just perhaps, one last puzzle worth solving.

She hadn't expected that puzzle to come with champagne, powdered wigs, and an impending corpse.

Which is why, when Lady Vera Everly swept into the room ten minutes late — all black velvet and pearls, flanked by gossip and disdain — Annabel watched her very, very carefully.

She'd seen enough in the Everly archives these past weeks — edited letters, charred corners, one curiously unsigned envelope — to know that Vera was planning something.

And when Lady Vera planned, people usually ended up furious, disinherited, or both.

Vera made her usual orbit, declined several toasts, made a single withering comment about a duchess's choice of brooch, and settled beneath the chandelier in a chair no one else dared claim.

She lifted her gin fizz.

And then she stopped moving.

***

One day earlier. Late evening. Everly House, Drawing Room.

Vera stood at the window, her silhouette outlined by firelight. The glass of port in her hand trembled — not from age, but from decision.

Clarissa Fairmont entered without knocking. She had once played Lady Macbeth in Stratford and never quite stepped out of character. She and Vera had shared a long, thorny friendship — part loyalty, part performance.

"You rang like a monarch. I assumed it was either treason or tea."

Vera didn't turn. "You're still here."

"I never leave before the curtain falls."

A pause.

"I'm changing the will," Vera said.

Clarissa inhaled sharply but kept her voice cool. "To Juliet?"

"To justice."

She turned, eyes gleaming like storm clouds.

"You always wanted the spotlight, Clarissa. But you never wanted the weight of it."

Clarissa's voice cracked. "You're doing this because I loved you."

"No. I'm doing this because I finally love myself enough to stop hiding."

Vera approached, placing a velvet pouch on the mantle.

"They're yours. For now. Keep them safe."

Clarissa didn't move.

"What if this goes badly?"

"It already has."

***

At first, it didn't look like anything at all.

Just Vera. Being still. Judging. Uninterested.

But Annabel's eyes were sharper than most. And she saw it.

The hand that didn't tremble. The glass that didn't tilt. The pearls — missing.

Evie was the first to speak. "Annabel."

"I see her."

"Is she—"

"Yes."

And that was when the screaming started.

Persephone stood.

Tail high. Ears alert.

She turned once, slowly, toward Annabel — and blinked.

We begin.

Chapter 2

The ballroom had shifted.

The glitter still sparkled; the strings still played — but now everything moved like it was underwater. Slower. Sharper. As if the murder had soaked into the walls and no one wanted to touch anything too hard.

Lady Vera lay still beneath a crisp linen cloth, draped hastily by a horrified footman. Her drink had been removed. Her chair had not.

Annabel stood nearby, watching the ripples.

People whispered. Gestured. Avoided looking directly at the body.

It wasn't grief. Not really. It was something more brittle, more self-conscious. Like embarrassment at the disruption of a well-planned evening.

Clarissa Fairmont lingered near the French doors — once Vera's closest friend, now the faded shadow in her mirror.

A woman in pink tulle nearly dropped her champagne. A footman caught it mid-fall, eyes wide.

"More like social self-preservation," Annabel murmured.

Evie handed her a fresh champagne flute and shrugged. "Dead duchess at a Versailles ball. Bit on the nose, really."

PC Tom Oakes had arrived — flustered, sweaty, and brandishing a notepad like it might defend him from the nobility. PC Oakes had been posted to Little Firling a couple of years ago after an unfortunate incident involving a lost swan and a broken antique vase in Devon. He was still recovering his dignity.

He approached with the puffed-up earnestness of someone very much out of his depth.

"Miss Deighton," he said, trying for authoritative. "If I could ask for your discretion—"

"Of course," Annabel said calmly, cutting him off with a smile sharp enough to slice a vol-au-vent. "You'll want names, movements, points of tension?"

Oakes blinked. "Well, I suppose, yes—"

"She was dead before dessert," Annabel continued. "Her posture never shifted. And she didn't touch her drink once."

She handed him a cocktail napkin with names scrawled in elegant script. "Start there."

Oakes stared at it like it had sprouted claws. Nodded dumbly. Shuffled away.

Evie sipped. "I love when you go full professor."

Annabel scanned the crowd, eyes sharpening.

Rafe Everly, the nephew — investment banker, professional eldest son — stood near the orchestra, face taut, tie askew. He wasn't looking at the body. He was looking at the solicitor, Mr. Grantham — and whatever they were saying, it wasn't condolences. Mr.

Grantham, the family solicitor, had been with the Everlys for nearly three decades — discreet, precise, and famously unbribable. Or so he liked to say.

"Rafe was furious at dinner," Annabel said quietly. "She toasted Juliet instead of him. It wasn't subtle."

"Neither was that snub at the heritage fund speech," Evie added. "She all but called him irrelevant."

"Perhaps he agreed."

Seraphina May, the art dealer — all cheekbones and curated charm — who once sold a Rothko to a duchess and a forgery to her dog, if rumour was to be believed — hovered by the staircase, speaking softly to two gallery patrons. She wore sequins like armour, and her smile was one shade too bright.

Annabel tilted her head. "She was Vera's 'special consultant,' yes?"

Evie snorted. "If you mean she helped launder emotions through curated canvases, then yes."

In the far corner, Juliet Everly stood alone — Vera's niece, quiet and elegant, long presumed ornamental. But not tonight.

Hands clasped. Expression unreadable.

She hadn't cried.

She hadn't moved.

Annabel's gaze lingered.

"She's hiding something."

"She always is," Evie replied. "But this time, it might be her moment."

Mrs. Gilchrist, the Everly housekeeper, swept past them with a tray she didn't need to be holding. Her face was unreadable. Her spine was military-grade.

"Her tea has never been poisoned," Evie whispered. "But if it ever is, she'll administer it herself."

And somewhere, winding quietly between ankles and furniture, Persephone moved like smoke. Watching. Listening.

Not leading.

Not yet.

Just listening. She absorbed the room, one blink at a time.

Annabel turned her gaze to the chandelier.

"No sign of struggle. No spilled drink. The pearls are gone. And so is the will."

Evie blinked. "The will?"

Annabel smiled faintly. "Oh, there's always a will, darling."

Chapter 3

The drawing room had been sealed, though the seal consisted of a single velvet rope and PC Oakes looking embarrassed.

Annabel stepped over both with ease, her presence both unassuming and undeniable.

Evie followed, offering the constable a nod that suggested he ought to be taking notes from her instead.

The room still smelled of lemon polish and tension. Mahogany gleamed, velvet drapes muffled the light, and everything had been arranged just so — as if Vera might still sweep in and reorder it herself.

This had been her sanctuary. Her throne room. Where decisions were made, gossip curated, threats whispered with clipped precision.

It was where Vera had held court, made pronouncements, and destroyed at least three marriages — two of them with only her eyebrows.

And now, it was too quiet — the kind of quiet that made you lean in, expecting something to shatter.

Annabel crossed to the writing desk and began to rifle — delicately, precisely. Not rummaging. Investigating.

"Look for what's missing," she said.

"You mean besides the gin fizz and her pulse?" Evie replied, flipping open a drawer in the side cabinet.

Annabel gave her a dry smile.

There was something intimate in this search — not invasive, not exactly. But it was a kind of mourning. Annabel had always believed that the way a person kept their desk was the truest biography. Vera's told a story of control, elegance, and the meticulous fear of being forgotten.

The drawers were tidy — too tidy. A sort of museum cleanliness that suggested preparation, or concealment.

She moved to the bookcase.e

Titles were arranged by genre, then author. A few volumes had been recently disturbed. A missing volume left a noticeable gap.

"Vera was exacting," Annabel murmured. "She wouldn't leave a gap."

Evie joined her, scanning the shelves.

"It's odd," she whispered. "No dust ring where the missing book was."

Annabel nodded. "Because it wasn't removed in a panic. Someone knew they were taking it — and planned for no trace."

Persephone hopped onto the piano bench and stared at the wall across from the fireplace.

Three minutes later, she meowed.

Annabel turned, following the cat's gaze.

Then frowned.

She stepped forward, fingers brushing against the painted panel.

Evie trailed her with curiosity.

The panel was subtly ajar.

Behind it — a hollow.

Inside, nestled in dust and velvet, a thin length of silk ribbon.

Annabel plucked it out and examined the faint imprint on the velvet.

"Pearls were here," she murmured. "Recently removed."

Evie knelt beside the panel. "And someone left in a hurry. That's a scuff."

She pointed to a faint mark in the wood — just barely visible where a shoe had dragged in haste.

Annabel tucked the ribbon into her notebook and glanced back at the empty velvet hollow.

"Why hide them here?"

Evie shrugged. "Why not a safe?"

"She wanted someone to find them. But not just anyone."

She touched the inside of the panel once more. The velvet was worn smooth. This hadn't been hidden recently — it had been used before.

Annabel turned to Persephone.

"Well spotted."

The cat blinked once.

A flick of her tail.

Of course.

Chapter 4

Clarissa Fairmont hadn't left the premises.

Which was a shame, really, because she had the air of someone who might confess to murder just for the drama of it. She wore black silk, had reapplied her lipstick with theatrical precision, and was presently holding court in the Everly library with three guests who hadn't yet realised the gala was definitively over.

When Annabel entered, Clarissa gave a tiny, amused smile, as if they were about to embark on an interview for the society pages rather than an informal inquiry into murder.

"I suppose you've come to ask me uncomfortable questions," she said, folding her legs elegantly.

"Yes," Annabel replied. "But I imagine you're more likely to volunteer something unhelpful."

Clarissa laughed, delighted.

"You know, I always liked you, Deighton. You're the only one who doesn't pretend to find me mysterious."

"Your opinion of me is inversely proportional to your standing with Vera."

Clarissa's smile froze for half a second. It was a good freeze — almost imperceptible — but it was there.

"I didn't kill her."

"No," Annabel agreed. "But you might know who wanted to."

Clarissa dropped into a chair with the theatrical grace of someone auditioning for a role no one had written.

"She changed the will," she said with a flourish. "Or was about to."

Annabel tilted her head slightly.

"She told you?"

"She told everyone — in her own way. That little speech about fresh starts. It was a warning wrapped in a toast. And Juliet looked positively seasick."

"To whom was she warning?"

Clarissa gave her a long, considering look.

"Anyone who depended on her. Financially. Socially. Emotionally."

Annabel leaned forward.

"And what were you, Clarissa?"

Clarissa's eyes glittered.

"Replaceable."

A pause.

Then, without ceremony, Persephone leapt into her lap.

Clarissa looked down at the cat, startled. "Even you, darling?"

Persephone blinked slowly.

Judgmentally.

Clarissa sighed.

"She said she was tying up the past. Getting her legacy in order. It frightened her, but she was determined."

Annabel watched her carefully.

"And the pearls?"

Clarissa hesitated.

"She had them. Said they belonged to the Everly matriarch — something about justice and shame. She didn't say more."

"And now they're missing."

Clarissa looked away.

"She wouldn't have misplaced them."

"No," Annabel said, rising. "But she might have baited a trap with them."

Chapter 5

Juliet Everly was not easy to corner.

But Annabel had spent a career coaxing revelations from students who thought silence was armour. And Juliet — with her stiff shoulders and distant gaze — was just another soul trying not to bleed.

Annabel found her in the conservatory, standing among orchids and moonlight. The air smelled faintly of jasmine, though something metallic lingered beneath it — a reminder that somewhere nearby, the house still carried the scent of death.

Juliet didn't turn when Annabel entered.

"Beautiful, aren't they?" Annabel said, stepping quietly beside her.

Juliet's voice was flat. "They're finicky."

"So was Vera."

Juliet's hands were clasped behind her back, white at the knuckles.

"She said she was tired of games. That she wanted to set things right."

"Did she say what that meant?"

"She said Rafe would understand."

"Did he?"

"She didn't get the chance to tell him."

Annabel waited.

Juliet turned slightly, face pale and composed.

"She told me she wanted to give me the gallery. Officially. Backed with trust funds and the deed to the east wing."

"That's generous."

"She said it was overdue."

"Was Rafe aware?"

Juliet's lips twitched into a tight smile.

"He's always aware."

Annabel looked at her carefully.

"She was going to name you her heir."

Juliet's composure cracked — a brief tremble in the corners of her mouth.

"I didn't want it. Not really. But I didn't want Hale to get it either."

Annabel stilled.

"Hale?"

"She never said it directly. But she kept alluding to someone — someone with long reach. Someone who could undo everything with a whisper."

"Rupert Hale," Annabel said quietly.

Juliet nodded.

"She said she was ready to stop being afraid."

"And then she died."

Juliet looked down.

"There was a man at the gala I didn't recognize. He was dressed as catering. Spilled champagne on her during the toast."

Annabel's pulse quickened.

"She reacted?"

"She looked at him like she'd seen a ghost. She didn't say anything. Just... stared."

"Did you tell anyone?"

"I thought it was nothing."

Annabel's voice softened. "And now?"

Juliet finally met her eyes.

"Now I think it was everything."

Chapter 6

The gardens behind Everly House had emptied, though the lanterns still burned as if reluctant to admit the party was over.

Annabel walked slowly along the path between the rose bushes, Persephone trotting ahead with the silent confidence of a queen inspecting her realm.

Evie joined her, carrying two lukewarm cups of tea and a new rumour about the duchess's second husband and a crate of missing champagne.

"I swear, this place breeds scandal like other towns grow tomatoes."

Annabel accepted the tea and nodded at Persephone, who had stopped beneath the ancient sundial near the herbaceous border.

She was staring at the base, tail twitching.

"Looks like we've got something," Annabel said.

Evie peered closer.

"A clue or a vole?"

Annabel crouched and ran her fingers along the edge of the sundial's stone base. It wobbled slightly.

Evie joined her, and together they shifted it aside.

Beneath, a hollow cavity.

Inside — a small velvet pouch, and a folded note, yellowed with time.

Annabel opened the note carefully.

It was written in Vera's hand. Sharp, angular, deliberate.

A diagram. A family tree. Circled names. And beneath it, one line in all capital letters:

"THE RING AND THE KEY."

Evie opened the pouch.

Inside: a signet ring bearing the Everly crest. And a small iron key, delicate and old.

"A key to what?" Evie whispered.

Annabel stood slowly.

"Something Vera didn't want Hale to find."

Evie paled. "So, it's true. She was going to expose him."

Annabel nodded. "She left breadcrumbs. This is one of them."

Persephone brushed against Annabel's leg, purring faintly.

"She always knew where to look," Annabel said.

"Cats or Vera?"

"Both."

Evie pocketed the key.

Annabel refolded the note.

And somewhere, beyond the hedgerows, the wind shifted — as if the garden itself exhaled.

***

The Hare & Hound pub smelled of cinnamon scones, wood polish, and smugness the morning after the gala.

Annabel and Evie slid into their usual booth near the window, where the light caught the flecks in Persephone's fur as she perched on the backrest, disdainful of the village chatter—but definitely listening.

"I give it till the end of the teapot," Evie muttered, "before someone casually drops a murder theory."

She was wrong.

It took exactly *three* sips of tea.

"That chandelier was never bolted in properly," said Mrs. Elspeth Muir, voice hushed but theatrically so. "I told my Harold when they hung it—'That thing's a death wish in crystals.'"

"It didn't fall, Elspeth," snapped Mr. Dunning from the fireplace. "She was poisoned. I saw her turn blue."

"Pearls were cursed," mumbled someone behind the scone display.

Annabel sipped her tea without looking up. "They've made it to the curse theory already. Impressive."

Evie leaned over. "Ten pence says we get a ghost rumour before the bill."

From the corner, young Maisie Fry—home from university and armed with a new fringe and a criminology minor—piped up: "I heard Juliet stood to inherit everything. And Rafe was *furious.* He knocked over an entire brandy tower!"

"She's not wrong," murmured Evie. "Brandy fountain *was* a casualty."

Mrs. Potts, the baker's wife, popped her head in. "And don't forget about the caterer boy. Not one of ours. Outsider. Said he 'forgot' the caviar. Suspicious, that."

"Probably Hale's doing," said someone ominously.

Persephone flicked her tail.

Annabel's eyes scanned the room. The village had absorbed the scandal the way it did all things — through crumbs, cough drops, and a barely suppressed appetite for mischief.

"Think they'll solve it for us?" Evie asked.

"No," Annabel said, standing. "But they might scare the killer into rushing."

Chapter 7

Ginny Pearce had been crying.

Not the wild, wailing kind, but the quiet, brimming sort that made her eyes red and her voice thready. She sat on a low bench near the back corridor, twisting a tissue into damp spirals.

Annabel approached slowly, with Evie just behind, holding a paper bag that contained, inexplicably, three scones and a half-empty thermos of mint tea.

"Ginny," Annabel said softly.

The girl looked up, startled. "Miss Deighton."

"You knew Lady Vera well?"

Ginny nodded, wiping her nose.

"She was... complicated. But kind. She paid for my evening courses. Said I had better things to do than polish silver."

"Did she confide in you?"

Ginny hesitated.

"She was tense, lately. Said people were watching her. That she didn't feel safe."

"Did she say who?"

"No. Just... she looked over her shoulder more than usual."

Evie handed her the thermos.

"She mention Rupert Hale?"

Ginny blinked. "Only once. She said he took what didn't belong to him and called it charity."

Annabel exchanged a glance with Evie.

"Did she give you anything?"

Ginny bit her lip.

"She gave me a letter. Said if anything happened to her, I should post it. But I... I lost it."

Evie tensed. "You lost a deathbed confession?"

Ginny shook her head quickly and fumbled through her handbag.

From a side pocket, she pulled out a small envelope.

"I never posted it. I couldn't decide if it was real or just... one of her moods."

Annabel took the envelope gently.

Addressed in Vera's looping script:

Mr. R.L. Grantham — Private & Confidential

Unsealed.

Inside: a second note. Longer. Typed. Signed in ink.

Annabel skimmed it. Then read it again, slower.

Her expression hardened.

"She names Hale. The pearls. The forgeries. Says she was ready to come forward."

Ginny looked miserable.

"I'm sorry. I didn't know it mattered."

Annabel folded the note.

"It matters now."

Chapter 8

Clarissa Fairmont was packing.

Not in a rush, not in a panic — but with a sort of tired grace, as if leaving had always been the plan, and she'd only been waiting for the right cue. Her travel case, monogrammed and well-worn, sat open on the chaise lounge. Silk scarves, leather-bound books, and one curious-looking opera mask were already tucked inside.

Annabel stepped into the room without knocking.

"You don't strike me as someone who flees."

Clarissa didn't look up. "I don't flee. I reposition."

Evie leaned against the doorframe. "Convenient timing, though."

Clarissa sighed and turned to face them. Her eyes were clearer than before. Sadder, too.

"She asked me to hold the pearls."

That got Annabel's full attention.

"She trusted you?"

Clarissa gave a rueful smile. "I was the distraction. She wanted someone obvious to take the fall if things went wrong."

"Did they?"

"I left my clutch on the sideboard during the third toast. When I went back, it was unlatched. The pearls were gone."

"Who knew you had them?"

Clarissa shrugged. "Anyone watching closely."

Evie frowned. "And what did she say when you told her?"

Clarissa's smile faded.

"I never got the chance."

Annabel moved closer.

"She planned to name Juliet her heir. The diagram in the garden hollow confirms it."

Clarissa nodded. "She thought Juliet had backbone. Said she was tired of men who mistook silence for strength."

"And you left that diagram out," Annabel said softly. "Where anyone could find it."

Clarissa stiffened. "I thought it would push her to act. I didn't mean—"

"But someone else acted first."

Persephone slinked into the room, her paws silent on the carpet.

She jumped onto the windowsill, curled her tail around her feet, and stared at Clarissa.

Not with scorn.

With pity.

Clarissa sat down slowly.

"I just wanted her to make good on her promises."

"She did," Annabel said. "In the end. But now it's our job to finish what she started."

Clarissa met her eyes.

And nodded.

The humans were loud.

They always were when one of them stopped breathing. Voices cracked, cups rattled, shoes squeaked. They filled the air with nonsense—fear, guilt, theories—none of it useful.

Persephone moved like smoke.

Under chairs, past spilt champagne, across marble that still carried the echo of Lady Vera's last steps.

She paused at the foot of the dais.

Sniffed.

Dust, gin, lavender, and...

Blood? No. Not fresh. Older. Faint. From behind the panelling.

She flicked her tail once.

Turned.

Out through the ballroom, past the frightened feet of a constable who reeked of biscuit crumbs and desperation.

The library was cooler.

Calmer.

She leapt silently onto the sideboard and stared at the fireplace. There it was again. The smell of silk and betrayal. The faint trace of Clarissa's perfume mixed with guilt.

But no danger.

Not *yet.*

She prowled to the piano bench. Sat. Waited.

It would come. It always did.

Persephone didn't solve murders.

She simply watched until the truth walked in.

And then she blinked.

Once.

Slowly.

The signal.

Let the clever one figure it out.

Chapter 9

The piano bench creaked as Annabel lifted the lid.

Inside: sheet music — mostly Debussy and Chopin — a small cloth pouch, and something wrapped tightly in navy velvet.

The faint scent of old perfume and varnish rose like a ghost.

Evie reached for it but paused, eyeing Annabel.

"Do we unwrap cursed objects before or after lunch?"

Annabel smiled faintly and unfolded the cloth.

A silver case rested inside. Rectangular, engraved with the Everly crest, and old enough to hum with secrets.

The metal was cool. Heavy. The sort of object that remembered being passed hand to hand in hushed rooms.

Evie raised an eyebrow. "Vera's private collection?"

"Let's see."

Annabel flipped open the case.

Inside: microfilm.

Evie leaned in. "Now we've gone Cold War."

Annabel carefully lifted the reel and held it up to the light.

"The labels match Everly estate appraisals. These are valuations — some of them altered. Others forged."

Evie exhaled. "So, she really had evidence."

Annabel nodded slowly. "And she'd begun gathering it. Methodically. Deliberately."

Her pulse picked up. Vera hadn't just been bitter — she'd been *preparing.* This wasn't paranoia. This was insurance.

She reached into the piano bench again and removed a note — a second one, folded neatly beneath the velvet.

It was short. One sentence, handwritten:

"He took what was mine. I'll take back what was stolen."

Evie frowned.

"Was she referring to Hale?"

Annabel was quiet for a moment.

The note felt colder than the case. Final. As if written by someone who'd already set the dominoes in motion.

"She must have known he'd retaliate."

"Then why do it?"

"She was tired. Of being manipulated. Of watching her family used."

Annabel looked up.

"She was preparing to fight back."

A sound behind them made them turn.

PC Oakes appeared at the door, a smear of pastry sugar on his sleeve and a very nervous expression on his face.

"Miss Deighton?"

"Yes?"

"There's someone asking for you. Says he was part of the catering team last night."

Annabel's eyes narrowed.

"Did you get a name?"

Oakes checked his notepad.

"Liam. Liam Harrow."

Evie straightened.

"Well, well. Let's go meet the champagne-spiller."

Chapter 10

Liam Harrow looked exactly like someone who wanted to disappear — thin, pale, and dressed in a jacket one size too big for his frame. His hands twisted together in his lap, and his eyes darted toward every window like they were escape routes.

The air in the parlour was still, but tense — like the room had paused to eavesdrop. Dust motes swirled in the afternoon light, ignoring the drama entirely.

Annabel studied him from across the room.

"You were at the gala."

Liam nodded.

"I was with the catering team. Plume Events."

Evie frowned. "We've checked — they don't exist."

"They don't," Liam said quickly. "I mean, they do. But not legally. I was picked up in a van with a sticker slapped on it. No ID. No names."

Annabel leaned forward.

"You spilled something on Lady Vera."

Liam swallowed.

"She brushed past me. I didn't mean to. She... she froze. Looked at me like I'd stabbed her."

"Did she say anything?"

"She said 'You.' Just that. And then she turned away."

His voice trembled on the word. Not theatrically — just enough to crack the air.

Evie crossed her arms.

"Who hired you?"

"I don't know. I got a text. Said it was a private job. Paid double in cash. Instructions were minimal. Wear black. Serve drinks. Keep quiet."

Annabel tilted her head.

"Did anyone else interact with you?"

"A man in a dark coat met me at the van. He gave me the uniform. Said I wasn't to speak unless spoken to. That's it."

Evie's voice dropped.

"You know who sent him."

"I think so."

Annabel gave him a long look.

"Rupert Hale."

Liam flinched.

"I don't know him. I swear. But people talk. And the man I saw at the back of the house when I left? That was him. Watching."

The name sat in the room like a shadow that refused to leave.

Annabel glanced at Evie.

"He's tying up loose ends."

Evie took a step forward.

"You're lucky Vera didn't scream. You'd be the body, not her."

Liam looked like he might cry.

"I didn't hurt her. I didn't even know who she was until the next morning. Please — I didn't do anything."

Annabel nodded.

"But you were a message."

Liam buried his face in his hands.

And outside, in the hallway, Persephone sat beside the door.

Waiting.

Listening.

As always.

Chapter 11

Seraphina May's gallery suite was as dramatically curated as her reputation — all exposed beams, soft lighting, and walls of minimalist paintings that cost more than an average holiday home.

She greeted Annabel and Evie in a robe of midnight silk, cigarette holder in one hand, disdain in the other.

"I assume you're not here to browse," she said, gliding toward them.

"No," Annabel replied. "We're here to discuss Vera. And the forged appraisals."

Seraphina's jaw tensed — just a flicker.

"I don't deal in forgeries."

"But you deal in acquisitions," Evie said. "And a lot of those pieces came through Everly channels."

Seraphina smiled thinly.

"Lady Vera was... eclectic in her tastes. She liked danger with her art."

Annabel stepped closer.

"She trusted you. She named you as her art advisor. That's more than taste."

Seraphina sighed and stubbed out her cigarette.

"She knew. About the pieces. Some were clean. Others... less so."

"Who pushed the dirty ones through?"

Seraphina hesitated.

"Hale. He owns part of the London gallery. Silent partner. Untraceable."

"And Vera found out?"

"She found out years ago. But she stayed quiet. Until recently. She said she wanted her legacy to be clean."

Annabel nodded slowly.

"She left evidence."

Seraphina's eyes widened.

"The microfilm."

"She hid it in the piano bench. Along with a note. She planned to expose everything."

Seraphina's face crumpled slightly.

"She said it would destroy me. And save Juliet."

Evie stepped forward.

"And the pearls?"

"I never saw them. But she talked about them. Said they were the key to realising something deeper. Family honour. Guilt. Justice."

"She baited the trap," Annabel murmured.

"And someone took it."

Persephone padded into the room.

Seraphina looked down at her.

"She never liked me."

Persephone blinked.

Then, slowly, hopped onto the windowsill — and curled up.

Observing with that particular disinterest that only cats — and very old souls — can manage.

Chapter 12

Mr. Grantham, the family solicitor, sat stiffly in the Everly study, his spine perfectly straight, hands folded atop a stack of manila files. He looked like a man who had spent a lifetime arranging secrets into tidy columns — and had just discovered one of them was missing.

The study smelled of old books and guarded silences. Sunlight crept across the edge of the rug like it wasn't sure it was allowed.

Annabel placed the envelope from Vera on the desk in front of him.

Grantham stared at it.

"She said she'd give it to you. In case anything happened."

He opened it slowly, reading in silence. His face didn't change — but something in his shoulders dropped.

"She knew," he said finally. "About Hale. About the forgeries. About the will."

"She told you she was making changes?"

"She said she was reviewing everything. Rafe. Juliet. The gallery."

"Did she name Juliet as heir?"

Grantham nodded. "Unofficially. The formal documents weren't signed. But the intent was clear."

Evie stepped forward. "And Hale?"

Grantham closed the envelope and set it aside.

"He's been circling Everly House for years. Buying up land. Pressuring institutions. He wanted a controlling stake in the estate."

"Why didn't Vera stop him earlier?"

"She was afraid."

He said it with no bitterness. Just fact. The kind of truth that had sat quietly in corners for years.

Annabel's gaze sharpened.

"But she wasn't afraid anymore. Not when she hid the pearls. The microfilm. The ring and key."

Grantham blinked.

"The key?"

Annabel produced it from her pocket, alongside the Everly signet ring.

Grantham paled.

His composure slipped — not a collapse, just a fraying at the edge. His hands tightened briefly, knuckles whitening.

"That key unlocks the trunk in my vault."

"And what's inside?"

"Original deeds. Proof that Vera's holdings were acquired before Hale's influence. A ledger. And... a letter."

Annabel's voice was low.

"A confession?"

"A naming. She writes that Hale was behind the death at the cliffs."

Evie drew a sharp breath.

"That was the first case," she whispered. "Your first case."

Annabel nodded.

"And we never had proof."

Grantham looked from the ring to the key.

"You do now."

Outside, a breeze moved through the hallway — and for a moment, it felt like the house exhaled.

Chapter 13

The garden was unusually quiet for midday.

Even the bees seemed reverent. Shadows dappled the stone path like lacework, and the air smelled faintly of lavender, earth, and the past.

Juliet sat on a stone bench beneath the wisteria, her posture as elegant as ever, but her gaze distant. A teacup rested beside her, untouched. The pearls of her earrings caught the sunlight in tiny, trembling flashes.

Annabel approached slowly.

"She wanted you to have it all," she said.

Juliet didn't turn. "She wanted too many things. Legacy. Peace. Revenge."

"She gave us the tools."

Juliet finally looked at her.

"But not the courage."

"She thought you had it."

Juliet gave a hollow laugh.

"She also thought I'd marry a baron and take up watercolours."

Evie appeared, holding a padded box. She opened it without ceremony.

Inside: the pearls.

They didn't gleam — they glowed. Softly. Like moonlight pooled in silk.

Juliet stared at them.

"She still had them?"

"She moved them. Re-hid them. Probably the morning of the gala. She was setting the trap."

"For Hale?"

Annabel nodded. "And for whoever might try to stop her."

Juliet's eyes filled — not tears, but some sharper emotion. Guilt. Grief. Resolve.

"She said she was done being afraid."

"She meant it," Annabel said.

Persephone padded up the path, her black fur catching no dust, her steps utterly silent. She stopped beside the bench and blinked at Juliet.

Juliet reached out — slowly — and the cat allowed a single stroke.

"She was always watching," Juliet whispered.

"She still is," Annabel said. "But now it's your turn."

Juliet took the pearls from the box.

They felt cool. Weighty. A truth worn around the throat.

"They belong to the house."

Annabel nodded.

"And you're the house now."

Above them, a petal drifted loose from the wisteria vine. It landed silently on Juliet's shoulder. She didn't brush it away.

Chapter 14

Clarissa Fairmont was drinking port in the gallery's north room, seated beneath a portrait of some long-dead Everly ancestor with too many medals and not enough chin. She looked smaller than usual. Or maybe just older.

The room was cold — not from temperature, but history. Even the velvet chairs looked judgmental.

Annabel took the chair opposite her.

"You could have told her."

Clarissa didn't flinch. "I did. She just didn't listen."

"You left the diagram where someone could find it."

"I thought it would scare her. Force her to act."

"It did," Annabel said. "Just not in the way you expected."

Clarissa sighed.

"She changed her mind. About Juliet. About everything. Said I'd had my time."

"She was right."

"I know."

Evie entered quietly, carrying a sealed envelope.

"We found this in her dresser. It was addressed to you."

Clarissa took it slowly.

Opened it.

Inside: a letter. No flourish. No farewell. Just a single sentence, written in Vera's sharp, slanting hand.

"You were never second — I just expected more from you."

Clarissa's breath hitched. Not loudly. Just enough to crack the air around her. She touched the edge of the paper like it might bruise.

"I loved her," she said.

"I know."

"She didn't love anyone."

Annabel tilted her head.

"She loved Little Firling. In her way. She loved the name. The house. The performance of legacy."

Clarissa gave a bitter smile. "And you. She admired you."

"She admired anyone who told her the truth."

Clarissa folded the letter and tucked it into her pocket.

"What now?"

"You help us finish what she started."

"Bring down Hale?"

Annabel nodded.

"You're a witness. A voice. A link to her past."

Clarissa stood slowly.

She looked taller now — not prouder, exactly, but less afraid of fading.

"I always wanted a role."

Evie smiled.

"You've got one."

Chapter 15

It came together faster than expected.

Rafe, once uncooperative, now provided access to financial records — partial, redacted, but telling. The catering contracts were traced to a non-existent branch of Plume Events. The catering van had expired plates. The driver, Liam, identified the man who had paid him in cash as "not the man's real name — but his eyes were cold."

And Vera's letter, sealed and now properly lodged with Grantham, was the final weight.

She named Rupert Hale.

Not with accusation.

But with certainty.

"He believes power is a form of inheritance," she wrote. "And so, I've taken back what was mine."

The words didn't rage. They didn't plead. They simply landed — heavy, final, unafraid.

PC Oakes arrived at the vicar's study just before lunch, holding the microfilm like it might bite.

"I've contacted the metropolitan fraud unit," he said.

Annabel nodded. "You'll need allies."

"I'll need a battering ram."

"You've got one."

She placed the ring and key on the table.

They didn't look like weapons. But Oakes took a step back all the same.

"The trunk in Grantham's vault confirms everything."

Oakes exhaled slowly.

"And you're sure this will hold up?"

Evie leaned on the windowsill.

"He's been protected for too long. But Vera laid the foundation. We're just finishing the house."

Oakes nodded.

Then turned to leave.

As he passed Persephone — seated like a gargoyle beside the tea tray — he hesitated.

She blinked at him.

Slow.

Ominous.

Like she'd judged him and found him... mostly tolerable.

Oakes straightened his collar.

And left.

***

The house was quiet.

Not peaceful. Waiting.

The kind of hush that comes before a storm — not in the sky, but in rooms where legacies are rewritten.

Juliet checked the lock on the side door.

Evie laid out the files on the drawing room table like weapons in velvet.

Annabel stood by the window.

"I didn't think it would be tonight," she said softly.

"They always come at sunset," Evie replied. "When they want to be seen."

Persephone, perched on the back of an armchair, twitched her tail once.

Then, headlights swept across the drive.

And the moment arrived.

Chapter 16

Rupert Hale arrived with no warning.

His car — sleek, black, and distinctly unsuited to Little Firling's cobbled lanes — pulled up outside Everly House just after sunset. The air inside had thickened, as if the walls themselves recognized an intruder.

He stepped out as if he owned the place. In a way, he almost did.

Annabel was waiting for him in the drawing room, Evie beside her. Juliet lingered near the fireplace, pale but steady.

Persephone sat atop the sideboard, tail curling like punctuation.

Hale didn't bother with greetings.

"I assume you think you've won."

"I don't play your game," Annabel replied. Her voice was calm, but her fingers curled tighter around the edge of the chair.

He laughed — sharp, joyless.

"Everyone plays. The difference is who knows it."

Evie stepped forward.

"Vera knew. That's why she left the letter. The evidence."

"She left paranoia."

"She left proof," Annabel said. "Deeds. Signatures. Microfilm."

Hale's jaw tightened.

"None of it holds up in court."

"But it holds up in Little Firling," Annabel said. "And in Parliament. And in the press."

Juliet spoke then — her voice clear, steady.

"You don't get to control us anymore."

Hale turned toward her, something flickering behind his eyes.

"Your aunt was always sentimental. She left you a mess."

"No," Juliet said. "She left me the house. And the truth."

Persephone stood. Her eyes, golden and gleaming, never blinked — the stare of something ancient, feline, and unimpressed.

She leapt down. Walked across the rug — and sat at Hale's feet. Looking up. Silent. Unblinking.

Hale flinched.

It was slight.

But it was enough.

And the room knew it.

Chapter 17

The arrest came three days later.

Not in the dead of night — Hale wouldn't have allowed that — but in the full glare of afternoon, with the press waiting at the bottom of the hill and Oakes standing straighter than he ever had in his life.

Forgery. Fraud. Coercion. Historical theft.

The charges read like the preface to a true crime bestseller.

Clarissa gave a statement. So did Grantham. Juliet submitted the family tree. Rafe, unexpectedly, verified the financial discrepancies. Even Liam — shaking and pale — testified by video call.

Annabel ran her fingers along the spines of the Everly estate records, their leather cracked like the surface of old secrets. Most volumes had been arranged with meticulous care — trust deeds, art appraisals, donation records. And yet, one folder didn't belong.

It was thinner than the others. No label on the spine. Stuffed between "Estate Expenses, 1981–1990" and "Gala Planning: Tricentennial Edition."

She pulled it out slowly.

Inside: a single torn page. Handwritten. Barely legible, but unmistakably Vera's.

"If anyone asks, he was never born here. He was never named. But if he comes back — you'll know him by the ring."

Annabel froze.

No date.

No signature.

Just a postscript, scribbled in the margin:

Don't tell Juliet. Not yet.

"Evie," she called.

Evie appeared in the doorway, holding a half-empty tin of mints. "Don't tell me we found a ghost heir."

Annabel held up the page.

"Not a ghost. But maybe a shadow."

Evie groaned. "I hate shadows. They're never straightforward."

"Neither is legacy."

Persephone, who had been curled in a window nook, opened one eye.

The look said: *Oh no, not again.*

Annabel folded the note, slid it into her pocket, and murmured, "Secrets always echo. Some just take longer to find their voice."

***

Annabel found Mrs. Gilchrist precisely where she expected: polishing the silver in the quiet of the back kitchen of Everly house at dusk, her posture as upright as the candlesticks.

"Miss Deighton," Gilchrist said without turning. "If you're here to talk about the will, I have nothing to add."

"I'm here about the ring," Annabel replied.

That made the polish cloth pause — for just a heartbeat.

"Lots of rings in this house."

"This one unlocks a vault. One Vera left behind. And a note suggesting someone else may have a claim."

Mrs. Gilchrist finally turned, her face as unreadable as the garden hedge maze.

"She never trusted banks," she said flatly. "Said the vault was only for things the living didn't know how to carry."

"And the boy?"

A silence thick enough to slice.

"She told me once," Gilchrist said slowly, "that not all debts are money. Some are names. Some are disappearances."

Annabel stepped closer.

"She hid a name."

"She *protected* one," Gilchrist corrected. "There's a difference. That boy was born under shame and silence — and Vera swore he'd never suffer for her mistakes."

"Was he Hale's?"

Gilchrist's jaw tightened. "He was hers."

No more. No less.

Annabel nodded once. "If he comes back?"

"Then you'd best pray he's nothing like his uncle."

She picked up the polish again and returned to her work.

***

Two days after the arrest, the first satellite van arrived by mid-morning.

By noon, there were six.

Little Firling, normally sleepy and floral, buzzed like a beehive poked with a boom mic.

A man in a tweed suit stood outside the bakery asking questions about "Lady Vera's last jam preference."

Three influencers filmed a #TrueCrimeWalk outside the chapel, one of them mispronouncing "Everly" four different ways.

Annabel watched from behind the lace curtain of the tea shop, sipping her blend and bracing herself.

Evie burst in, winded and indignant. "One of them just tried to interview Persephone."

Annabel didn't blink. "Is he still alive?"

"Barely. Scratched the living truth out of his forearm."

They stepped outside together.

A Daily Truth tabloid reporter attempted to corner them.

"Miss Deighton! Can you confirm the pearls were cursed? And were you romantically involved with the inspector?"

"I am," Annabel said, "deeply committed to my kettle."

They kept walking.

Behind them, Persephone strutted down the path like a general returning from battle.

Someone snapped a picture.

She growled.

The camera short-circuited.

Annabel smiled.

"Little Firling doesn't do circus," she said.

Evie adjusted her sunhat. "But it does do clean-up."

***

The pearls were recovered. Not from Hale, but from a hidden compartment in the catering van, found abandoned near a farm on the outskirts of Lincoln.

Juliet had them polished and mounted in a museum-style display in the Everly gallery.

"On loan," she told the press. "From the estate. For the people."

Persephone was given the position of unofficial gallery guardian, though she preferred the west windowsill and growled at anyone who tried to photograph her.

Annabel returned to her cottage with a new set of notes, two thank-you baskets, and the quiet satisfaction of puzzles completed.

Evie resumed her role as village archivist — part detective, part historian, full gossip.

And for the first time in weeks, Little Firling exhaled.

The spring sun softened. The garden bloomed.

And the village settled back into the hum of secrets not yet uncovered.

Epilogue

Annabel sipped her tea on the back porch, a wool shawl over her shoulders and a crossword tucked under one elbow. The crossword was only half-finished — something about birdwatching slang and obscure British biscuits — but she was more focused on the view.

The garden was humming again. Not whispering, not brooding — just humming. Birds argued in the hedges. A bee flirted with a dahlia. The world, for once, was not keeping secrets.

Evie emerged from the cottage with a box labelled "ARCHIVES — DO NOT BURN," muttering about the lack of alphabetization in the local history logs.

"Someone once filed a sea monster sighting under *Cabbages,*" she announced. "We are a nation of lunatics."

Persephone sat atop the railing, tail flicking lazily, her eyes closed in a sunbeam. She was not asleep. She never slept when mysteries were afoot — only rested her eyes in judgment.

"I've been thinking," Annabel said.

Evie paused. "Oh dear."

"We should make it official."

"The podcast?"

"No, the register. A proper one. The Little Firling Puzzle Archive. A living log of all unresolved oddities, possible crimes, and curious folk tales."

"With ribbons?"

"And index cards."

Evie grinned.

Persephone stretched.

Then, with great drama, the cat turned her head toward the gate.

A postman was approaching. Not their usual one — this man walked with careful posture, as though carrying fragile secrets instead of packages.

He handed Annabel a slim parcel. No return address. Just a wax seal stamped with what looked like a brushstroke and a question mark.

Evie peered over her shoulder. "Looks like someone wants us at that art retreat after all."

Annabel opened the parcel.

Inside: a sketch. Delicate. Wild. And in one corner, half-erased — the shape of a face no one had yet named.

Persephone leapt down.

She sniffed the paper.

Then turned sharply toward the rose trellises, ears twitching.

Annabel rose.

Another whisper.

Another secret.

Another brushstroke on the canvas of Little Firling.

She turned to Evie.

"Shall we?"

Evie picked up her notebook.

Persephone trotted ahead.

And together, they stepped into the next mystery.

***

Persephone walked alone beneath the wisteria.

The village was sleeping. Humans dreamed their muddled dreams, cluttered with memory and nonsense. But the night air whispered clearer truths — rustling leaves, distant fox prints, and the scent of change drifting in like sea fog.

She moved like ink in water.

Silent. Certain.

The Everly House loomed behind her, heavy with the echoes of what had been buried, revealed, rearranged.

She paused beneath the sundial.

Sniffed.

Something lingered in the earth there — old metal, ribbon silk, the last trace of Vera's will not yet read.

Persephone sat. Watched. Waited.

From across the fields, wind tugged at the hedgerows. Somewhere, an owl called — low and warning.

Persephone did not answer.

She was not prey.

She was the watcher between worlds. Between candlelight and clue. Between tea trays and truths.

Tomorrow, the humans would return to routines.

Annabel would misplace her reading glasses again. Evie would mutter about poor filing systems. The kettle would whistle. The archive would yawn.

But something else was coming.

The cat could feel it.

A ripple beneath the rose trellis. A sketch left unfinished. A lie whispered in turpentine.

Persephone rose.

She turned toward the east, where the morning would rise behind the hills, and walked — not hurried, not hunting, just *ready.*

Because peace was only a pause.

And someone would soon forget that Little Firling remembers everything.

Especially the cat.